Charmed Life
Caitlin's Lucky Charm

Also by Lisa Schroeder

Charmed Life

It's Raining Cupcakes

Sprinkles and Secrets

Frosting and Friendship

Charmed Life

Caitlin's Lucky Charm

LISA SCHROEDER

SCHOLASTIC INC.

No part of this publication may be reproduced, stored in a retrieval system, or transmitted in any form or by any means, electronic, mechanical, photocopying, recording, or otherwise, without written permission of the publisher. For information regarding permission, write to Scholastic Inc., Attention: Permissions Department, 557 Broadway, New York, NY 10012.

ISBN 978-0-545-60372-0

Text copyright © 2014 by Lisa Schroeder
All rights reserved. Published by Scholastic Inc.
SCHOLASTIC and associated logos are trademarks and/or registered trademarks of Scholastic Inc.

12 11 10 9 8 7 6 5 4 3 2 1   14 15 16 17 18 19/0

Printed in the U.S.A.   40
First printing, June 2014

The Bracelet

The Pink Giraffe.

How could any eleven-year-old girl possibly resist a name like that?

But the name wasn't the only reason Caitlin, Mia, Libby, and Hannah stopped outside the quirky little boutique. The whimsical, carnival-inspired window display featuring fashionable mannequins standing next to an old-fashioned popcorn cart, a cotton candy machine, and a giraffe from a carousel also intrigued them.

The four girls had spent the afternoon exploring Main Street during their field trip into town. It'd been the first time they'd left Camp Brookridge since arriving at summer camp five weeks earlier. They'd had lots of fun, browsing the shops and eating sweet treats. But time was running out, and the girls had yet to find the special something they were looking for: a trinket that symbolized their friendship.

The campers stood there, admiring the window display for a moment before Caitlin said, "I think this might be it. Come on. We have to hurry."

"Wait!" Mia said. "I want to take your picture first. In front of the window."

The others were used to this by now. Mia took pictures of everything. They quickly posed with big smiles while pointing at the window display, and Mia snapped the picture.

Once inside the boutique full of charming clothes, jewelry, and accessories, the girls scattered like mice.

Mia, a strong and athletic Latina girl from Southern California, spotted a display of jewelry inspired by the sea. She fingered a pair of silver earrings in the shape of sand dollars.

Libby, a petite girl with big brown eyes who had come all the way from a town outside of London, England, almost squealed when she saw a jewelry case with the sign TEA PARTY RINGS. Each ring featured an intricately painted teeny-tiny teapot or teacup.

Hannah, tall and lanky, was a quiet but funny girl from

Tennessee. She admired a display of neon T-shirts with zoo animals doing human activities such as riding a bike, skateboarding, and making a pizza.

And then there was Caitlin, the outgoing and friendly African-American girl from Connecticut. Caitlin was the one who had come up with the idea to find something special that sealed their friendship. With that thought firmly on her mind, Caitlin made her way to the back of the shop, knowing that's often where sale items could be found.

The girls didn't have a lot of money, even if they pooled what they had together. When Caitlin saw an antique bookcase filled with various items and a sign at the top — 50 PERCENT OFF — that's where she decided to look.

It didn't seem like much, really — one lonely bracelet on a plastic jewelry holder with a few sad charms lying in a dish next to it. Caitlin and her best friend from home, Jade, loved making jewelry together, and they'd made some pieces that were much prettier than this simple design. But there was something about this bracelet that made Caitlin want to try it on. She slipped it off the holder, unhooked the clasp, and then slipped it around her wrist.

As she pieced the clasp together, a memory popped out of nowhere. It was the first time all four girls had sat together at dinner, the second day at camp. The chef served fruit pizzas for dessert. None of the four girls had ever heard of fruit pizza — let alone tasted it — with a cookie crust, a custard filling, and fresh fruit laid out on top. They bonded over that delicious dessert and talked about it for days afterward.

"The bracelet looks pretty on you." Caitlin looked to her left and found a petite saleswoman with lots of wrinkles and short gray hair watching her.

"Oh, thank you," Caitlin said. "Can I show it to my friends?"

The woman waved her hand and said, "Of course. Let them try it on too, if they'd like. That lucky feeling of knowing it's right doesn't happen simply by looking, does it?"

Caitlin swore she saw a twinkle in the woman's eye as she said the word *lucky*. She hurried over to Libby near the front of the shop, unfastening the bracelet as she went. "Here, I want you to try this on. And tell me what happens."

Libby gave Caitlin a strange look. "Happens? What do you mean?"

"Just wait and see," Caitlin said as she grasped Libby's hand, slipped the chain around her wrist, and secured it.

Libby fiddled with the bracelet, staring at it for a moment, before she looked up and met Caitlin's eyes. "It was so strange. I saw the four of us, sitting around the campfire, singing our favorite song. You know, the one about the bear." She leaned in and whispered, "Did that happen to you?"

"I saw something different," Caitlin replied. "But yes, as soon as I fastened it, I had a happy memory of the four of us."

Just then, Mia and Hannah walked up. Mia pointed to a clock on the wall. "We need to go. Like, now."

"Wait, I found the perfect thing for us," Caitlin said, pointing to Libby. "It's a charm bracelet."

"Not just any charm bracelet," Libby said. "It seems to be . . . special."

"Special?" Hannah asked. "Does it sing or something? I'll tell you what, my grandma thinks those birthday cards that sing when you open them are the funniest things ever."

Caitlin smiled. "No, it doesn't sing." She remembered what the saleswoman had said. "I think it might be lucky."

"Lucky?" Mia asked. "How do you know?"

"We'll tell you later," Libby said as she unhooked the bracelet. "Do we have enough money?"

"Yes," Caitlin said. "Barely. I wish we had enough to buy a charm too, but we don't. Maybe we can take turns wearing it and add charms to it later?"

"Awesome," Mia said.

"Great idea," Hannah chimed in, reaching over and fingering the bracelet. "I love how it feels nice and strong." Her eyes got big and round, like it suddenly made perfect sense. "Just like our friendship!"

The girls walked to the cash register, where a young woman with curly blond hair sat on a stool, flipping through a magazine. After Caitlin set the bracelet on the counter, the girls all reached for their wallets.

"Where's the other person who works here?" Caitlin asked. "I wanted to thank her for her help."

The young woman looked up from her magazine. "I'm the only one working this afternoon."

Caitlin glanced around the shop, but she didn't see anyone else. "So who was the older woman with short gray hair?" She looked at her friends. "You saw her, didn't you?"

They all shook their heads.

"Must have been another customer who snuck out when you weren't looking," the young woman said.

"Hm. Yeah," Caitlin said. "That must be it."

As the four girls made their way back to the bus with the newly purchased charm bracelet tucked away in Caitlin's backpack, Caitlin glanced behind her, feeling as if someone was watching them.

But she didn't see anyone there.

Chapter 1

Sunflower
Sure to brighteN up your day

<u>CAMP JOURNAL, DAY 41</u>

I've said it before and I'll say it again.

Camp Brookridge ROCKS.

I can't believe I have to go home tomorrow. Home, where there's no horseback riding. Home, where there's no lake to swim in. Home, where there are no Cabin 7 friends to hang with.

When I came here, I hoped I would have fun, but never in a million years did I imagine how much I would ♥ this place and the friends I've made.

Mia, Libby, and Hannah are just the best!

I don't want to think about tomorrow. It hurts too much.

When the music rang out over the loudspeakers, letting campers know that reflective time was over and free time had begun, Caitlin slammed her journal shut. She jumped off her bed and reached down to get the tiny satin pouch from her suitcase that held the special bracelet along with the three headbands she'd made earlier in the week during arts and crafts. Some of the girls she shared a cabin with rushed past her, toward the door, talking and laughing, many of them wearing swimsuits.

She looked around for her three friends and spotted them back in the corner, by Libby's bunk, so she made her way there, stuffing the small items into her pockets.

Libby lay on her bottom bunk, curled up on her side. Mia and Hannah stood on either side of the bed.

"Hey," Caitlin said. "What's going on? If we don't go now, we won't have much time."

"Libby's sad," Mia said. "She said she's going to skip friendship circle today. She doesn't want to bring us down."

Caitlin took a seat on the bed and put her hand on her friend's knee. "Oh, Libby. I know. I hate thinking about leaving tomorrow too."

Libby gave a little nod as tears spilled from her eyes. "I'm going to miss you guys so much."

Caitlin pulled Libby up and gave her a long hug. When they separated, Caitlin said, "We'll write to you. And you'll see, the year will zoom by. It'll be July again before you know it. Then we'll all be together again."

"I'm going to write you lots of letters," Mia said. "So many, your mailman will want to break my fingers. Wait, is it called a mailman in England?"

Libby smiled as she wiped her face with the back of her hands. "It's a postman. I just wish my aunt and uncle weren't so strict. No phone or any other electronics until I'm thirteen. It's not fair."

A few weeks earlier, Libby had shared with Caitlin and her other closest camp friends that she lived with her aunt and uncle because her parents were killed in a car crash when she was four. Caitlin had felt terrible for her, but Libby had said there was no reason to feel bad. Her aunt and uncle had been very good to her, and she loved them like she would a mom and dad.

"What about a computer?" Hannah asked.

"Only if it's for homework," Libby replied.

"I'd be upset too," Caitlin said. She stood up, looking back and forth between Hannah and Mia. "You know, I really don't want Libby to feel left out. What if we make a pact to only write each other letters?"

"It sounds so hard," Mia said. "Do you think we could stick to it?"

"We haven't given each other our phone numbers, since we aren't allowed to have phones here," Hannah pointed out. "So, before we leave, we just exchange our addresses and nothing else. I kind of like the idea. It makes me think of the box of notes my mother kept from when she was in high school. They didn't have texting back then. She said they passed notes in the hallway and sometimes even in class. And just think, she can keep those notes forever and ever."

Libby's eyes lit up. "Forever. Wow. I love the sound of that."

"That's it, then," Caitlin said with a smile. "Only letters. Or, you know, postcards." She gently pulled on Libby's hand. "Come on. Let's go to friendship circle. It's our last one, and remember, we're doing an offering today. You don't want to miss that, right, Lib?"

"Okay," Libby said as she scooted off her bed. "Let me grab what I need."

The girls split up to collect the things they wanted to take with them and then met at the door of the cabin. Once outside, they took off running. They ran across the open grassy area toward the far side of camp.

Behind the arts-and-crafts building was a small hill. Caitlin was the first to reach the top. Breathing hard, she looked down at the other side and smiled when she saw the three huge pine trees planted close enough together that they created a circle among them.

Mia had been the one to find the cozy little spot with a shaded canopy of pine branches on the second day at camp, during free time. She showed them the spot the day after the four became friends over the fruit pizza. It had been Caitlin's idea to name it the friendship circle. And every day since they'd claimed it as theirs, the girls had used it during free time to share everything from snacks to journals to secret wishes and dreams.

Now, the girls made their way down to the trees and took their spots inside. Caitlin looked around at the others and told herself to stay upbeat. She took a deep breath and smiled. She looked at Libby, wanting to make sure she was doing all right.

"Go on," Libby said. "Start the meeting the proper way. I'll be fine."

"Welcome to another meeting in the friendship circle," Caitlin said. She was always the one who started off the meeting. "As it's been since the beginning, our friendship circle is secret, safe, and special. Speak your mind, but please be kind. And always remember . . ."

The rest of the girls joined in. Usually the words were

spoken loudly and with enthusiasm. But not today. They said the words not only quietly but with a hint of sadness as well. "No matter what, wherever we go, we're friends forever, this we know."

"I think the first order of business," Caitlin said as she took the red sachet from her pocket, "is to figure out who takes home the lucky bracelet."

Caitlin carefully pulled out the bracelet and put it in the palm of her hand. It glistened against her dark skin. Hannah reached over and picked it up, then held it out in front of her, letting it dangle in the air.

"It looks so sad without any charms," Hannah said. "Like a dog without a bone. Like a rosebush without buds. Like a —"

"Okay, okay," Mia said. "We get your point. We'll just have to add to it all year long, so by next summer, it'll be a true charm bracelet. Caitlin, I think you should take it home. You're the one who found it."

The other girls nodded their heads in agreement.

"But Libby's upset," Caitlin protested. "Maybe having the bracelet would make her feel better."

"No," Libby said. "I want you to have it. You found it, but that's not all. You're really the one who brought our group together. Remember, that second night before dinner, how you asked the three of us if we could sit together? That took a lot of courage. I don't know how you knew the four of us would get along so well, but somehow, you did."

Caitlin shrugged. "I wanted to get to know each of you for different reasons. Mia seemed to always be smiling, so bouncy and full of life. And I loved the way she said *awesome* all the time."

Mia grinned. "Awesome. That's me!"

The girls laughed.

Caitlin continued. "And then there was Libby, with her adorable British accent and the way she helped everyone make their beds that first morning. Tucking the corners in tight and everything."

"What can I say, my uncle likes a well-made bed," Libby said. "He got it from my grandpa, who was in the military."

"But it was so nice of you to help every single girl in our cabin," Caitlin said. She turned and looked at Hannah. "And then there was the quiet girl from Tennessee. She may not talk much, but when she does, she makes people smile."

"My daddy always says laughter is the best medicine," Hannah said. "And there were a lot of homesick girls those first few days. Including me." She looked at Caitlin. "Libby's right. You brought us together. You should take it home first. Give me your arm."

Caitlin did as she was told. As Hannah fastened the bracelet in place, Caitlin closed her eyes, just for a couple of seconds.

"Did it happen again?" Libby asked.

"Yep," Caitlin said. "I saw the four of us sitting around the little table in Sally's Sweet Shop, eating ice cream cones during our field trip."

"We were meant to have this bracelet, y'all," Hannah said. "I bet it's luckier than a four-leaf clover. Luckier than a shooting star! I just know it's going to help us have a good year, filled with lots of luck."

"And before we know it," Libby said, "we'll be back together again, here at Camp Brookridge. Charm Sisters."

"Charm Sisters," the three other girls repeated, as if on cue.

And then they all laughed.

Chapter 2

Forget-Me-Not
in other words, remember me forever

"How long should I keep the bracelet?" Caitlin asked.

Mia piped up. "It'd be cool if we each got to have it a couple of times throughout the year. So maybe a month or two?"

"That sounds good," Caitlin said. "Okay, it's time to answer our friendship circle question of the day. Pass your journal to the person on your left, since we passed to the right yesterday, and answer the question, 'What are you most looking forward to when you get home?'"

The girls passed the journals around and started writing. The rule was each girl had three minutes to answer the question of the day. They'd decided early on that by answering in someone else's journal, they'd learn interesting things about one another.

Caitlin wrote in Libby's journal:

Q of the day: What are you most looking forward to at home?

Making chocolate chip cookies and eating them ALL. Oh, and also sleeping in my bed, which will be quite lovely. (See how I sound British there?) I'm going to miss you, Libby. I think you're sweet like licorice. First I sound like you, and then I sound like Hannah. Seriously, what am I going to do without you guys?

Your Cabin 7 BFF,

Caitlin

When they finished, they passed the journals back to their original owners.

"Now it's time for our friendship offering," Caitlin told the girls.

"Oh no," Hannah said sadly. "Our last friendship offering."

"Come on, do you *want* to make us cry?" Mia asked Hannah.

Caitlin continued. "You know the drill. Put the items you brought with you in the middle of the circle."

This part of friendship circle was Caitlin's favorite. It'd been Hannah's idea to bring something once a week to share with one another. The girls often made things in the arts-and-crafts building like pot holders, painted rocks, and little clay pots, and some of those items had been offered up in weeks past.

Sometimes the items weren't the kind you could keep though. One time, Libby had brought all four of her lip gloss tubes and a compact mirror, so the girls could try different flavors. Another time, Caitlin shared a small book of children's poetry she'd had since she was a little girl. She'd brought it along to camp to read, in case she got homesick. After she'd put it in the circle, the girls had passed it around so each one could read a poem out loud.

Now, no one spoke as each girl gathered her items. It was as if the girls knew the silence made the moment all the more special.

Caitlin reached into her shorts pocket and pulled out the headbands. They were made out of nylon cord and braided, in three different colors. One was daffodil yellow, another one poppy red, and the third one hydrangea blue. She placed them in the middle of the circle.

From her little backpack, Mia took out something

wrapped in paper towels. When she pulled the corners back, the girls saw she had brought brownies, the exact same ones they'd had in the dining hall the night before. Mia set the brownies in the circle.

Hannah opened her journal and tore out three pages, one at a time, and folded them before placing them in the circle. At the top of each page was one of the girl's names, written in Hannah's prettiest cursive handwriting. "You can't read these until you're on your way home," she whispered.

And finally, Libby placed three of her barrettes into the middle of the circle. She often wore the cutest barrettes to keep her pretty blond hair from falling in her eyes.

The girls took turns until all of the items had been picked up.

"Can we eat our brownies now?" Libby asked.

"I think we should," Hannah said. "Chocolate will make us feel better."

"And just think, we still have to get through the final campfire tonight," Caitlin said as she picked up her brownie. "Seeing who gets awards will be fun, but I'm afraid the rest will just be . . ."

"Sad," Libby said. "I know. I overheard the counselors

talking. They're going to ask campers to stand up and share their favorite memories."

"Let's all share funny ones," Mia said. "Like, I think I'll share the time when the fat squirrel chased Hannah into our cabin."

"Oh, that's a good one," Libby said, smiling. "What did you do to make the squirrel so upset with you, anyway?"

Hannah laughed. "Nothing, I swear. Remember, I told y'all he was just sitting there, by the tree outside our cabin, and he looked so sweet. I wanted to get as close as I could, and then he started running. But instead of running away from me, he ran toward me. It was crazy!"

Caitlin laughed. "Then you came screaming into the cabin, like you were being chased by a pack of wolves or something."

"I had nightmares for days about that evil squirrel," Hannah said with a shudder.

Everyone laughed.

When the music started playing a moment later, indicating free time was over, they all grew quiet. Caitlin looked around at the circle, wishing she could make time stop. She didn't want to go. Mostly, she didn't want to have to say good-bye tomorrow. She took in each of her friends, wanting to capture the moment in her mind forever.

Libby, like a sweet and dainty violet.

Mia, like a strong and bold sunflower.

And Hannah, like a bleeding heart, tender yet lively.

Don't cry, don't cry, don't you dare cry, Caitlin told herself as she slipped Hannah's note along with the barrette from Libby into her pocket. The other girls put their things away as well, and then, as Libby stood up, she held out her hands for Caitlin and Mia to grab as they got to their feet.

Caitlin reached down and helped Hannah up. Then the four of them stood there for a few seconds, hand in hand, underneath the canopy of the pine tree branches. The warm summer breeze kissed their cheeks as they turned to go, and Caitlin couldn't remember a time when she felt so happy and so sad all at once.

Chapter 3

Bird of Paradise
a very strange flower

Dear Caitlin,

On the first day of camp, you came over and said hi to me. You were the very first person I met. I'll always remember that. You were soooo nice to me.

I was terrified that I wouldn't make any friends. I know I've told you guys about how I really didn't want to go to camp. I thought I'd rather go to Mars instead of New Hampshire, because I'd probably fit in better on Mars. Now I have to go home and tell my parents they were right and I was wrong, because going to summer camp was the best thing that's ever happened to me. And you were a big reason for that.

I'm gonna miss you like the moon would miss the stars if they decided not to twinkle in the night sky. Please, please, PLEASE write to me. A lot!
Your Cabin 7 BFF,
Hannah

As Caitlin finished reading Hannah's note from their very last friendship circle, she thought about the award she'd been given at the final campfire. Friendliest Camper — the only one that was voted on by every single girl at camp. When Caitlin's camp counselor, Deena, had presented the award to her, she'd said that although Caitlin had her core group of friends, campers said again and again that she'd been helpful and kind to everyone she came in contact with during her six weeks at camp. Deena said she'd heard stories about Caitlin pitching in to help someone with a craft project or assisting with chores when it wasn't even her turn.

Along with a certificate, the counselors had given her a special flashlight to say thank you for being one of the bright lights at camp. "Keep shining," Deena had said as she handed it to her.

Being friendly wasn't something Caitlin thought about

really. It's just how she was. She liked doing things and meeting people and helping out when needed. Getting the award made her hopeful that maybe things at the Arts and Communications Magnet Academy (ACMA for short) she'd been accepted to wouldn't be so bad. If most of the girls at her camp had seen her as friendly, hopefully kids at her new school would too.

"What are you reading?" Isaac asked Caitlin, snapping her back to reality. Her eight-year-old brother sat next to her in the family's minivan.

"None of your business," Caitlin said, sticking the note back in her pocket.

"Is it something from your new *boyfriend*?" Isaac teased.

"It was an all-girls camp, genius," Jessi, their older sister, said from the backseat behind Caitlin and Isaac.

"Well, maybe she snuck out in the middle of the night and found a boyfriend," Isaac said. "Charlie said that's what they do at camp. Sneak out in the middle of the night. Did you do that, Caitlin? And if you did, were you scared wolves or bears might eat you?"

"That's enough, little man," their dad, Mr. Rogers, said as he looked at the kids in the rearview mirror. "I'm sure she did not sneak out at night. And Caitlin's right. You don't need to be getting into her personal business."

Their mom, Mrs. Rogers, turned around from the passenger seat and looked at Caitlin. "You okay, honey? You haven't said much. I know you had fun, since your letters told us so. You sad to be leaving?"

Caitlin nodded and looked out the window. "Yeah. It was hard saying good-bye to my friends."

Hard didn't even begin to describe it. Once they'd said their tearful good-byes after breakfast, Mia, Libby, and Hannah had gotten on a camp bus to go to the airport, where they'd catch their flights home. Caitlin was the only one of the four who lived within driving distance. Camp Brookridge was about three hours from her home in Connecticut. She'd felt a little jealous of the three of them getting to spend more time together on the bus, though she knew they'd all have to say good-bye eventually.

"Where'd you get the barrette?" Mrs. Rogers asked. "Never seen you wear anything like that before."

Caitlin instinctively reached up and touched Libby's gift. Her mom was right; she didn't usually wear anything in her hair. But she'd clipped it in that morning, because it seemed like the right thing to do.

"You need a trim, don't you?" Mrs. Rogers said. "I'll get an appointment scheduled for you next week before school starts."

"What about school shopping?" Caitlin asked. "I really need some new jeans. All of mine are too short."

Her mom looked at her dad before she replied. "We might have to wait a month or two before we do that. The weather will still be nice for a while. You can wear shorts and skirts, right?"

Caitlin was so shocked by that response, she could hardly think straight. Did her mom really say she had to wait for new clothes? They always went clothes shopping the last week of summer. It was as much of a tradition as having waffles with strawberries on the first day of school. Did her mother actually expect her to wear clothes from last year on the first day? Who did that?

"Dad, I'm hungry," Isaac said. "Can we stop and get cheeseburgers?"

"Ew," Jessi said. "You know I'm vegetarian now, Isaac. Find someplace where I can get a salad. Okay, Dad?"

"We're not stopping," he called out. "Your mom packed sandwiches for all of us."

Confused, Caitlin looked at her little brother. He just shrugged his shoulders, like he didn't know what was going on either. Their mother never brought food along on a road trip. Why do that when it was easier to stop on the way?

That's what fast-food places were for — and they never got to eat at them any other time.

"Okay, is someone going to tell me what's going on before I start screaming to strangers on the highway that I've been abducted by aliens?" Caitlin said. "First we're not going school shopping like we have every year since Jessi's been in school, and then Mom actually packed sandwiches for us to eat?"

"Yes, they're in a bag in the way back," Mrs. Rogers said. "There's also a little cooler filled with bottles of water. Can you please start passing stuff around, Jessi?"

"Mom," Caitlin said. "Please. Enough about the sandwiches. What is going on?"

It was quiet for a moment before Mr. Rogers finally replied. "I suppose we should explain. Your mother and I have decided to tighten our belts."

"What does that even mean?" Caitlin asked. "Are you going on a diet?"

Mr. Rogers laughed. "No." He rubbed his stomach, which wasn't exactly flat. "Though I could probably use a few less cheeseburgers in my life, now that you mention it."

"Caitlin, wake up," Jessi said, leaning forward and slapping her sister on the shoulder. "Don't you get it? We're broke. We don't have any money. That's what he means."

"We're not broke," Mrs. Rogers said with a sigh. "I really don't want you kids to worry. Don, please reassure them. Tell them everything's fine."

"It is fine," he agreed. "But things at work aren't exactly smooth sailing right now, so we're socking away money just in case."

"In case you get fired?" Isaac asked.

"He's not going to get fired," Caitlin said. She bit her lip. "Are you, Dad?"

"Let's put it this way," Mr. Rogers said. "My plan is to stay employed. Now, whether I work for my current company or a different one, we'll have to wait and see. Jessi, you got those sandwiches? I'll take a turkey with cheese, please."

Caitlin reached over and fingered the bracelet, hidden underneath the sleeve of her hoodie. Maybe it could bring some luck to her family, she thought. She didn't want her dad to lose his job. He worked at the hospital in town, as a manager in the accounting department. And although Caitlin didn't know exactly what his job entailed, she knew he didn't complain about it very much, and he seemed to like the people he worked with.

Once everyone had their sandwiches, Mr. and Mrs. Rogers started talking among themselves about a neighborhood meeting coming up. Caitlin looked at her turkey sandwich and decided she wasn't very hungry.

Isaac leaned toward his sister while he munched on his peanut butter and grape jelly lunch. He looked up at her with his big brown eyes and long eyelashes. "Caitlin, I'm scared," he whispered. "I don't want us to be broke. I'll really miss french fries if I have to eat sandwiches forever."

She patted his scrawny little leg. "It'll be okay," she told him. "You and I can go for french fries sometime this week, how'd that be?"

"You got some money?" Isaac asked.

"Yeah, I have a little bit. Enough for some fries, anyway."

Suddenly, Caitlin felt guilty about spending the money her parents had given her for camp. They probably needed it now and wished they could get it back from her. What would they say if they saw the bracelet? Would they be upset she'd spent money on something that wasn't even entirely hers?

Nah, they'd understand. Wouldn't they?

Chapter 4

Carnation
comes in a rainbow of colors

When Caitlin walked into her house for the first time in six weeks, she stopped cold. The faint smell of fresh paint hung in the air as she stared in disbelief at the maroon walls in the family room. It was quite a change from the white walls they used to have.

"Do you like it?" Mrs. Rogers asked. "I painted just about every room in the house while you were gone."

"What? Why?" Caitlin asked.

"After fifteen years, it needed to be done. I really wanted to get new furniture and window coverings too, but with the uncertainty of your father's job, this was all we could do right now. What do you think?"

"It's very . . . red," Caitlin replied, not wanting to hurt her mom's feelings. She thought it made the room look really dark.

"But doesn't it look nice with our black leather furniture?" Mrs. Rogers said. "I wanted to find a way to give each room a makeover without spending a lot of money."

For months before Caitlin left for camp, her mother had been obsessed with shows on the decorating channel, especially one called *Spiffy in a Jiffy*. Now Caitlin knew why; her mother must have been planning this project for a while.

"Hold on," Caitlin said. "You didn't paint my room, did you?"

"No, I knew you'd want to choose the color, so I waited for you to get home. I'd like to get it done before school starts though, so tomorrow we'll go and pick out the color and then you can help me."

Caitlin groaned. "Do I have to? Mom, I just got home."

"I know you did, but I want to get this done."

"How long does it take?" Caitlin asked. "To paint a room?"

"It's an all-day project, at least," she said. "So don't make any plans for the next couple of days."

Caitlin's whole body slumped. That was not the answer she wanted to hear. After all, she had e-mails to read. Television shows to watch. As much as she'd enjoyed camp, she'd been looking forward to getting back to the technology she'd gone without for six weeks. And then there were those chocolate chip cookies she wanted to bake.

"Painting is really fun," Isaac said, who had come in and sat down on the couch. "Can I help, Mom?"

"Sure you can," she said. "You did a great job helping me with your room."

"Does Caitlin have to go through all of her junk like I did and decide what she wants to get rid of?" Isaac asked.

"Yes, she does."

Caitlin didn't want to hear any more. It made her exhausted just thinking about all the work she'd have to do in the coming days. Or maybe it was the fact she'd hardly slept the night before. The Cabin 7 girls had whispered into the early morning hours, and since it was their last night, the counselors hadn't stopped them.

Mr. Rogers came through the door, carrying Caitlin's suitcase and tote bag. He set them down. "Here you go, Peaches. I'm guessing laundry is in your future today, huh?"

"Great," Caitlin mumbled. "And the fun just keeps coming."

"Where's Jessi?" Mrs. Rogers asked.

"She went to her room," Isaac said.

"Caitlin, when you go upstairs, will you remind her that

tomorrow night we're volunteering at the soup kitchen? I want to make sure she doesn't make any plans."

Caitlin shook her head, confused. "Soup kitchen?"

"You've heard of a soup kitchen before, right?" Mr. Rogers said. "It's a place where people go when they're down on their luck and need a good, hot meal for free."

Caitlin looked at her mom. "What do you mean, we're volunteering?"

"I mean," Mrs. Rogers said, "that we're going to help out by cutting up vegetables, serving food, wiping down tables — whatever they ask us to do."

Caitlin suddenly felt like she'd been transferred from summer camp to work camp.

Her mom continued. "While our belt-tightening may be a bit painful, I want us to remember we have a lot to be thankful for and that there are others a lot worse off than we are. We'll leave here around four thirty so we can check in there at five o'clock. Okay?"

Caitlin could only nod before she said, "I'm going to my room. I'll start unpacking."

"Good idea," her mom said.

Caitlin dragged her stuff upstairs and stopped at her sister's room, where she knocked on the door.

"Come in."

She opened the door and peeked in. Jessi was sitting on her bed, looking at her phone. "Mom said to remind you that we're volunteering at the soup kitchen tomorrow night, so don't make any plans."

"Too late," Jessi said. "I'm not going."

Caitlin raised her eyebrows. "You might want to go downstairs and tell her that, because I have a feeling she's not going to be too happy with you."

"Nah," she said. "It'll be fine. I'm not worried about it."

"Whatever," Caitlin mumbled as she shut the door.

When she got into her own room, she shoved the stuff inside, shut the door, and fell down onto her bed, face-first. At last, something felt normal.

After she lay there for a few minutes, she rolled over and grabbed her phone off the nightstand. Totally dead. Of course it would be. She found the charger and plugged it in to the wall and watched it come to life.

She had a few texts from friends, the most recent one from Jade, Caitlin's best friend since kindergarten, who lived just down the street. This would be the first year they wouldn't be going to the same school, since Caitlin was transferring to the magnet school. Butterflies fluttered in her stomach at just the thought.

After she sent texts letting her friends know she was alive and well and home, she set the phone down and looked at her suitcase with dread. If she were still at camp, reflection time would be up next on the daily schedule, which meant thirty minutes of reading or writing or anything that could be done quietly. Caitlin and her friends had decided it had really been a chance for the counselors to get a few minutes of peace and quiet each day. At first, the girls had thought it was ridiculous, being forced to stay on your bed and be quiet. But after a few days, Caitlin had started to look forward to that time. And as her journal pages filled up, she knew someday she'd be glad she had her memories written down to look back on when she was missing camp and her friends. Like now.

Caitlin rummaged through her stuff until she found the journal she'd received on the first day of camp. The day after they'd gotten the journals, the girls had spent an afternoon in arts and crafts decorating them. Caitlin's journal had the words *BE UNIQUE, BE YOURSELF* on the cover. She'd found a magazine with a full-page advertisement for a new brand of jeans called Unique, with those four words as the ad header.

Now, Caitlin flopped back on her bed and flipped through the pages of her journal until she found the page she was looking for.

CAMP JOURNAL, DAY 22

Q OF THE DAY: WHEN YOU'RE IN A BAD MOOD, WHAT DO YOU DO TO CHEER YOURSELF UP?

I GO SURFING IF I CAN. THERE'S SOMETHING ABOUT BEING IN THE WATER WITH THE SUN ON MY SHOULDERS AND THE WIND ON MY FACE THAT MAKES EVERYTHING FEEL RIGHT. BUT IF I CAN'T FOR SOME REASON, HERE'S WHAT I DO. I PUT ON A SONG AND I DANCE. I DON'T LET ANYONE SEE ME, BECAUSE I AM NOT A GOOD DANCER, TRUST ME. BUT IT HELPS. LET ME KNOW IF YOU EVER TRY IT!

YOUR CABIN 7 BFF,
MIA

Caitlin grabbed a pen from her nightstand, turned to the last page, and started writing.

CAMP JOURNAL, DAY 42

I'm home. At least, I think I'm home. Things look kind of different, and my family is acting really different. Maybe aliens have invaded their bodies. I don't know. All I know is everything seems weird!!

I keep thinking about Mia, Libby, and Hannah. Wondering where they are, what they're doing and if they might actually hold the luck instead of this bracelet I'm wearing since nothing about today seems lucky AT ALL.

I'm bummed there's no friendship circle this afternoon. Instead, there will be the unpacking of the suitcase followed by laundry followed by looking around my room trying to figure out what I'll keep and what I'll give away. Wow, so much fun in one day I don't know if I can handle it.

I'm thinking maybe I should have a dance party by myself before I start in on that unpacking. . . .

Caitlin went over to her small stereo and turned it on. She flipped through the radio stations until she found a song she liked, and then she let loose.

She moved and grooved, waving her hands and sliding her feet.

When the song was over a couple of minutes later, she flopped back on her bed, her heart pounding inside her chest.

"What do you know," she whispered with a smile. "It worked. Thanks, Mia!"

Chapter 5

Daffodil
Spring's best friend

"Rise and shine, Caitlin, because we are going to shop until we drop!"

Caitlin opened one eye, wondering if she was dreaming. Her eye landed on her favorite poster — a photo of one lonely yellow flower shooting up through the crack in a sidewalk. She looked down at the clock next to her bed. It was just a little after nine o'clock.

Nope. Not dreaming.

She sat up and found Jade standing there. At least, she thought it was Jade standing there.

"Wow," Caitlin said. "Look at you."

Jade grinned as she patted her shoulder-length black hair, now done up in a bunch of tiny braids. "Do you like it?"

Caitlin rubbed her eyes. "It's super-cute!"

"I know, right?" Jade took a seat on the edge of the bed. "I'm so glad you're home. I missed you! Did you miss me?"

Caitlin yawned. "Yes. Like a sad cupcake without any frosting."

Jade laughed. "Summer camp made you a poet. Very sweet."

"Actually, I think my friend Hannah made me a poet." Caitlin stood up, pulled her dad's extra-large T-shirt she wore down to her knees, and peeked through the curtains to take a look outside. It was raining.

"A great day to go to the mall, huh?" Jade said, standing up and joining Caitlin at the window. "Come on. Go shower and get dressed. My mom said she would take us in an hour, so we can be there when everything opens."

Caitlin yawned again. "I don't think I can go with you."

Jade stuck out her bottom lip. Caitlin had seen her do it too many times over the years.

"Please, not the poochy lip," Caitlin said. "You know the poochy lip makes me feel bad. There is nothing more I'd love to do than go to the mall with you. But my mom is making me go to the store and pick out paint."

"For what?"

Caitlin waved her arms around. "To paint my room.

Didn't you notice when you came in? My mom was a painting machine while I was gone. Lucky for me, she waited until I got home to do my room. I might have ended up with something like army green."

"Huh. I didn't notice." Jade clapped her hands together. "Probably because I was just so excited to see you."

Caitlin wrapped her arms around Jade and gave her a hug. Then she went to her dresser and pulled out some clothes. "I'm glad you came over. Things were weird yesterday."

"Weird? What do you mean?"

"Everything is just really different around here. My dad's worried he might lose his job. My mom's turned into Martha Stewart or something. My sister's suddenly a vegetarian and seems to kind of hate us all." Caitlin sighed. "Like I didn't have enough stress in my life with starting a new school."

"Is it too late to change your mind?" Jade asked her. "About the new school, I mean."

"Probably," Caitlin said. "And, you know, I really do want to go there, because the kids are mostly creative types. It seems like a good place for me. But what if I'm wrong, and I don't make any new friends? Like, what if I'm miserable there?"

Jade put her hand on her hip. "Caitlin, that's so silly. You're so sparkly, and everyone loves you. You'll be fine."

Caitlin smiled. "Thanks. I hope you're right." She turned toward the door. "I'll be right back. With fresh breath and an empty bladder."

Jade laughed. "Okay. I'll be here."

When Caitlin returned a few minutes later, she found Jade had made her bed for her.

"Wow, you should come over every morning and wake me up," Caitlin told her friend. "You wanna come down and have breakfast with me?"

Jade shrugged. "Okay. What are we having?"

"How about cinnamon toast?" Caitlin said as she grabbed a Chapstick and went to work putting some on her lips. "With hot cocoa."

"Mmm, that sounds good." Jade walked toward the door and then stopped in front of Caitlin. "Hey, what's this?" She reached out and touched the charm bracelet. Caitlin hadn't taken it off since she'd been home.

"Oh, I bought it on the field trip into town, with my three friends from camp. We're going to buy charms for it and take turns wearing it."

"See?" Jade said. "If you made friends like that at camp, you'll make friends like that at your new school."

Hopefully Jade was right. It made Caitlin feel better just hearing her say it, anyway. She took the bracelet off and stuck it, along with the Chapstick, into the pocket of her jeans, not wanting anyone else to see it for now. It was hard explaining it to people, and no one would understand how much it really meant to her except her Cabin 7 friends.

After the two girls had made their toast and cocoa, they sat down at the kitchen table. Caitlin's mom came in a few minutes later.

"Got her out of bed, I see," Mrs. Rogers said. "Good work, Jade."

"Thanks. She couldn't resist my charm and good looks, even in her sleep."

It made Caitlin laugh.

"Maybe I should have you wake up her sister next," Mrs. Rogers said.

Jade shook her head. "Nope. No way. I'd like to leave this house alive, please."

"Where's Isaac?" Caitlin asked, wondering why she hadn't seen him wandering around, being his cute-but-annoying self.

"Charlie invited him over to his house for the day," her mom said. "That way we can go shopping for paint and start prepping your room so it's ready to paint tomorrow or the next day."

Caitlin held back a groan and gave her mom a big smile, trying to stay positive about the whole thing. "That sounds great! I just can't wait!"

Jade ate the last bite of her toast and pointed at Caitlin. "Look at that, you really did come back from camp as a poet."

"Don't I know it," Caitlin said.

"You're so funny," Jade said. "And I am so glad you're back."

Caitlin stood in the aisle of the home improvement store looking at the pile of paint sample cards she and her mother had collected. When Caitlin had said she wanted light blue, she had no idea there were about a hundred and one choices of light blue.

Robin's-Egg Blue.

Summer-Sky Blue.

Turquoise Blue.

And that was just a few of them.

"Can't I take the money you're going to spend on paint and buy a new outfit instead?" Caitlin asked. "I'm fine with keeping my room the way it is."

"I'm using coupons," her mom told her. "It's not going to cost very much. You wouldn't have enough money to buy an outfit, trust me. So which color do you want?"

Caitlin didn't want a can of paint. She wanted something new to wear on her first day at a brand-new school. How come her mom couldn't understand how hard this was going to be? A new outfit might help her feel better. Make her feel like she had at least one thing going for her.

Maybe she could ask Jade if she could borrow something. Except, what could she say that wouldn't sound pathetic? "Jade, can I borrow something to wear on the first day of school because my parents are afraid they're going to be broke and refuse to buy me anything?"

Caitlin sighed and flipped through the samples one more time. "How about this one? I like the color, and I especially like the name. Bluebell. You know, like the flower."

"Oh, that's lovely." Her mom read the name. "And the perfect choice for you, isn't it?"

Her mom knew how much Caitlin loved flowers and that she dreamed of owning a flower shop someday. To Caitlin, it sounded like the best job in the world, making up beautiful, colorful arrangements for people.

"All right," Mrs. Rogers said. "Let's buy our paint and

get home so we can go to work. We need to move all the furniture out, except for your bed, because we'll wait and do that tomorrow so you can sleep there tonight. Then we have to put masking tape all around the baseboards and window. After that, we'll . . ."

As they walked to the register, her mom kept talking, but Caitlin tuned her out. She was thinking about the squirrel feeder they'd passed at the end of one of the aisles. It made her smile as she thought of Hannah and the evil squirrel that had chased her at camp. If only she had some money, she could buy it and send the feeder to Hannah. It would have made her laugh so much. She just knew it.

Caitlin's heart ached a little bit at the thought of her friend. She missed her. All of her camp friends, actually. She put her hand in her pocket and felt the bracelet there, safe and sound. It made her feel a little bit better. In a way, they were always with her. Now, if the bracelet would just start doing its thing and bring a little luck Caitlin's way. Or at the very least, bring an amazing new outfit Caitlin's way.

Chapter 6

Peony
the perfect centerpiece flower

"This doesn't look like a soup kitchen," Isaac said as they walked through the church doors the following evening.

"How do you know?" Caitlin asked him. "You've never even seen one."

"The kitchen is this way," Mrs. Rogers said, pointing. "Since the church isn't in use during the weekdays, they let volunteers use the kitchen and parish room to serve meals to people who need one. It's a nice thing to do, don't you think?"

Isaac slipped his hand into Caitlin's as they walked downstairs, following a sign that said OUR DAILY BREAD SOUP KITCHEN.

"I'm scared," her little brother whispered. "What if they make me cook soup? I don't know how to make soup."

Caitlin sort of knew how he felt. She wasn't scared so much as a little bit nervous about the whole thing. What would they be doing, exactly? And what if people wanted to talk about their problems? Was that part of working there too?

"It'll be okay," Caitlin told Isaac. "They aren't going to make you do anything too hard. And we'll be right there to help you."

"This is ridiculous," Jessi mumbled under her breath, so their mom couldn't hear her. Jessi had been told she would come along to the soup kitchen or her cell phone bill would go unpaid indefinitely. Since *indefinitely* probably meant *forever*, or at least a very long time, Jessi gave in and agreed to come. But she was making it completely clear she would much rather be just about anywhere else.

They walked through the parish room, where lots of long tables were set up. Caitlin noticed that each table had a centerpiece of flowers, which made the room seem bright and cheerful. As they made their way toward the kitchen at the far end, Caitlin noticed whatever was cooking smelled really good. Like lemon and spices.

Once in the kitchen, they met the lady in charge, Mrs. Watson, who wore bright pink lipstick, had silver hair that was almost blue, and wore a big, round button on her apron that said FRIENDLY EAR, RIGHT HERE. She smiled and seemed truly happy to meet every member of Caitlin's family. When she shook Caitlin's hand she said, "You're a real friendly one, aren't you?"

Caitlin felt her cheeks get warm. "I guess so. I mean, hope so."

Mrs. Watson slapped her leg and said, "I knew it! I have a sixth sense for these kinds of things. I could see it in your eyes. The eyes are a window into the soul, you know."

Caitlin wasn't sure what that meant exactly, so she just smiled and nodded her head. Mrs. Watson introduced the Rogers family to the other volunteers. Caitlin felt funny when she realized they were the only kids there. But Mrs. Watson continued to try and make them feel welcome.

"I'm so glad to have you here," Mrs. Watson said to the four of them as she handed out red aprons. "After you wash your hands and put on your plastic gloves, I'm going to put you to work preparing the salad dressing and buttering bread. Sound good?"

"Sure," Mrs. Rogers said for all of them. "Whatever you need us to do is fine."

Caitlin and Isaac teamed up with the bread, knives, and butter, while their mom and Jessi went to work preparing the small cups of salad dressing. For thirty minutes, Caitlin and Isaac buttered bread until they had four trays full.

"That was fun," Isaac said. "And easy. Can I have a piece of bread now, Caitlin?"

"No," she whispered. "It's not for us, it's for the people who come here and are hungry."

"But I *am* hungry," Isaac said.

"We'll have dinner when we're finished, okay?"

Mrs. Watson came up to them and said, "Would you two mind passing out the bread and cookies as people come through the line?"

"Sure," Caitlin said. "We can do that."

"Great. I'll put you down at the end. Each person will get a piece of bread and a cookie after they've gotten their lemon chicken with pasta and salad."

Isaac rubbed his stomach. "That sounds good. And they get all that for free?"

Mrs. Watson laughed. "Yes. And you know what, Isaac? For being such a good helper, I'll put aside a cookie for when you're done, how's that? We have plenty."

"Is it chocolate chip?" Isaac asked.

"How'd you guess?" Mrs. Watson said. "That's my favorite. How about you?"

Isaac nodded.

"Okay, come down here and get ready," Mrs. Watson said, leading the way. "I'm going to go and open the doors, and then it'll be real busy for a while. I know you kids will do a good job at being kind to these folks. After all, a lot of them are hungry for more than just food."

"What's she mean, Caitlin?" Isaac asked after Mrs. Watson left. "What else are they hungry for?"

"Shhhhh, Isaac, not now." The truth was, Caitlin wasn't exactly sure what Mrs. Watson had meant either.

People started streaming through the doors at the other end of the parish hall. The volunteers took their places by the food they were serving and started dishing it up as people came through the line.

Caitlin wasn't sure what she had expected exactly, but the people all looked . . . normal. There were old people, young people, single people, and families. Some had light skin; some had dark skin. It reminded Caitlin of going to the mall and seeing all kinds of people there. Mostly what she noticed here was how grateful everyone seemed to be. She listened as people came through the line, and they often didn't say thank you just one time but to every single server.

Isaac and Caitlin started making a game out of saying, "You're welcome" at the same time. It made some of the people laugh.

There was one old man who made all the volunteers ooh and aah as he came through the line to get his food. "That's Sonny," the lady serving salad next to Caitlin explained. "He's here five nights a week, just like we are. We don't usually allow pets in here, but we make an exception for Sonny. The thing is so small, he just keeps him in his jacket the whole time."

At first Caitlin didn't know what the lady meant by "the thing." But when Sonny got down to their end of the line, all was revealed. Tucked into the man's green Windbreaker was a white dog, its tiny head barely peeking out.

"Hello," Sonny said to Caitlin and Isaac as they put a piece of bread and a cookie on his plate. "I don't believe I've had the pleasure of making your acquaintance. I'm Sonny, and this here is my little friend, Wilbur."

"Like the pig in *Charlotte's Web*," Caitlin said.

"That's right," Sonny said. "One of my favorite books. I used to work in an elementary school, you see. Keeping the place clean. The library was my favorite place. And what are your names?"

"I'm Caitlin, and this is my brother, Isaac," Caitlin replied.

"What kind of dog is that?" Isaac asked. "Or is it a puppy? It's so tiny."

Sonny moved aside so he didn't hold up the line. "He's a miniature Chihuahua. Come by my table when you're done serving everyone, and you can pet him, all right? He's a friendly sort, just like the two of you."

"Cool," Isaac said. "See ya later."

Isaac looked up at Caitlin. "This has been a lot more fun than I thought it would be."

Caitlin smiled. "You know what? You're right." She turned around to see what her mom and sister were up to. They'd been put to work washing dishes. When Caitlin's eyes met Jessi's, her sister glared at her.

If her sister hadn't been in such a bad mood, the afternoon would have been just about perfect.

Chapter 7

Bluebell
adorable and comforting

The bluebell walls in Caitlin's room looked fantastic.

She couldn't believe how nice the room had turned out. Yes, it'd been a lot of work prepping the room and going through her stuff so they could get rid of things she didn't want or need anymore. But when it was all done, she absolutely loved everything about it.

When they'd finished, Caitlin's mom let her do all the things she'd been dying to do since she got home. She baked cookies. She watched television for three hours straight. She checked e-mail and played on the computer.

Mrs. Rogers took all the kids for haircuts and bought them new socks, underwear, and one pair of shoes each. But nothing else.

"Hopefully in a couple of months," their mom kept saying.

Now, as Caitlin lay on her bed, admiring her freshly painted walls the night before her first day of school, she thought maybe she would just stay in her beautiful room forever. After all, you don't need new clothes if you stay in your room all the time. You don't need anything, really. Not even friends.

She'd written letters to Hannah and Libby and was finishing up the third one, to Mia.

Last year, when I told my mom I wanted to try and get in to the arts and communications school, she asked me if I had thought it all the way through. Yes, I told her. I want to go there. Everything I love — reading, writing, art — is there in a much bigger way than the regular middle school. I said to her: I feel like I belong there.

Now I'm wondering, WHY did I think I belong there? I have no friends there. I belong with my friends. I belong with Jade, who I've eaten lunch with every day since we first started going to school. How can I possibly eat lunch without her? Who will I eat lunch with at the new school? And how does that all work? Do I just sit down somewhere and hope I've picked the right group of kids? What if I pick the mean kids and they ignore me? Or worse, throw my lunch across the cafeteria?

When we were painting my room, my mom told me everything will work out. That it might be hard at first, but in a couple of months, my new school will feel like home. I hope she's right.

I'm wearing the bracelet tomorrow, hoping it brings me lots and lots of luck. If I can find friends half as sweet as you, Hannah, and Libby, I'll be happy.

Your Cabin 7 BFF,

Caitlin

She stuck the letters into three envelopes and pulled out her camp journal to get their addresses. That happy camp feeling washed over her as she flipped through her journal. She stopped and read a question of the day.

CAMP JOURNAL, DAY 10

Q of the day: Do you have any pets?

I have a Scottish terrier, also known as a Scotty dog, named Dexter. He loves people but hates other dogs. He likes going on walks, but we have to be careful if we pass another dog, because he growls and acts like he wants to fight. I wish I could ask him why he does this. I hope you don't think Dexter is a mean dog. He's not, I promise. He's very sweet. I just think he gets scared sometimes and so he puts on this tough-dog act.

Your Cabin 7 BFF,
Libby

Caitlin thought back to Wilbur, Sonny's little dog. All three kids thought he was the cutest dog ever. Of course, all the way home Isaac whined about how much he wanted a dog. As much as Caitlin liked the idea, she knew their house didn't need one more thing to worry about right now.

After the envelopes were all addressed, she put them on her dresser, telling herself to ask her mother to mail them tomorrow. She went to her closet for the approximately one hundred and forty-fifth time, opened the doors, and began to search for the perfect outfit to wear the next day.

The perfect outfit would say, *I'm cool in an artistic sort of way.*

The perfect outfit would say, *I'm happy to be here and would love to be your friend.*

The perfect outfit would say, *I do not look like I was pulled out of the closet from Caitlin's pathetic wardrobe that is so last year.*

That's when she had the idea to go look in someone else's closet. Nothing in hers appealed to her. At all.

She knocked on Jessi's door. "Go away," Jessi said. "I'm busy."

"Can I look in your closet?" Caitlin asked. "I don't have anything to wear tomorrow."

"Nope. They wouldn't fit you anyway. I'm bigger than you."

Caitlin opened the door and peeked in. Her sister was sitting on her bed with drawings laid out all over.

"What are you doing?" Caitlin asked.

Jessi gathered up the papers. "None of your business. Didn't you hear me? I said no."

"Please?" Caitlin begged.

Jessi shook her head. "Go ask Mom. She'd probably let you."

Caitlin gave her a dirty look. "Because her clothes would totally fit me while yours don't, right?"

Jessi shrugged.

Caitlin shut the door and stood in the hallway, trying to

decide what to do. Looking in her mother's closet was totally lame, wasn't it?

But I'm desperate, she thought.

She went to her parents' room. "Mom?" she called out. No answer. Caitlin went into her mom and dad's walk-in closet. She ran her hands along her mother's sweaters and blouses. Not a single thing looked like anything she would want to be seen in.

"This is crazy," she mumbled.

As she turned around to leave, she spotted her dad's tie rack. He had a lot of ties. A manager practically lives in ties. She noticed he had two red ties that were identical. *How funny,* she thought. She pulled them off the rack and looked at them.

Red was a bold color. Confident. The ties were silky smooth, and Caitlin liked the way they felt in her hands. She put them around her neck and knew that would never work. If she was going to use them for something, she needed to be original. Unique. A trendsetter!

With the ties in hand, Caitlin went in search of her parents. They were both sitting on the couch, her dad reading a book and her mother engrossed in another episode of *Spiffy in a Jiffy.*

"Dad, did you know you have two red ties that are exactly the same?" Caitlin asked.

"Yes," he said. "And the funny thing is, I hate red ties."

"Can I have these then?" Caitlin asked.

"Sure. Knock yourself out."

"What are you gonna do with them?" her mom asked.

"I don't know. Got any ideas?"

"Actually," she said, "I think I saw something on the Internet about how to make two ties into a belt with a bow that you wear around your waist."

Caitlin gasped. "Mom! That would be so cool. Can we look for it? Will you help me?"

"Yes. As soon as this show is over, I'll help you."

She could see it now. Everyone would want to know how Caitlin had managed to make a belt with her dad's ties. That belt would be the talk of the school, which meant Caitlin would be the talk of the school and she would have a group of friends in no time. Maybe even an entire army of friends.

She plopped down next to her mom, smiling. The lucky bracelet was finally working. She just knew it.

Chapter 8

Buttercup
loves to dance in the wind

*T*he belt with a bow was super-cute with a black skirt and white shirt. At least Caitlin thought so. But no one else at school seemed to even notice Caitlin or her one-of-a-kind belt.

She went to homeroom first period, sat down, and waited for the bell to ring. A group of four girls came in chatting and laughing, and Caitlin felt a little tug on her heart. That's what she wanted. To have friends like that. To be in a group like that.

If only my Cabin 7 BFFs were here.

The group of girls sat toward the back of the room. Caitlin suddenly felt ridiculous, sitting in the front row. Why had she done that? No one sat in the front row unless they had to. She got up and moved to the back, sitting down next to one of the four girls. This one had pretty green eyes and the most shiny, wavy red hair she'd ever seen. Caitlin thought she looked like Ariel in *The Little Mermaid*.

"Hi," Caitlin said to her. "I have to tell you, I really love your hair. It's just so . . ."

Caitlin paused. The girl gave her a funny look. "Red?" she asked.

"Well, no," Caitlin said. "I mean, it is, but I was going to say shiny. Except that sounds weird, to say to a perfect stranger, your hair is so shiny, you know? I was trying to think of a different word. But I couldn't think of anything. I guess I could have said beautiful, because it is totally beautiful, but that probably sounds weird too."

The girl gave her a weak smile and then turned around to talk to her friends.

Caitlin could feel little beads of sweat popping up on her forehead. The girl must be wondering what planet Caitlin had come from, Caitlin thought. What was that mess of words that had just spilled from her mouth? It was like she had no control of what had come out.

Caitlin decided she had to try again. She had to show this girl that she was not as strange as she'd just sounded.

"Hey," Caitlin said, reaching over and tapping the girl's elbow. The girl turned and looked at Caitlin. She did not look too happy. In fact, she looked kind of mad. "I'm sorry. That all sounded strange, I know. I'm Caitlin. I don't know anyone going to this school, so I'm just really nervous."

The girl gave her a little nod. "Oh."

"What's your name?" Caitlin asked.

"It's Brie," she said.

"Like the cheese?" Caitlin asked. "That is so awesome. I love cheese. I bet if that were my name, I would walk around hungry all the time, with cheese constantly on my brain. I mean, not that I think about myself all the time, that would be weird, right?"

Caitlin swallowed hard. *Okay, stop it,* she told herself. *Just stop it. Do you want this girl to think you are completely crazy?*

Brie gave her a funny look. "Riiight."

The bell rang, saving Caitlin from any further humiliation. She wanted to crawl into a hole and stay there. But, since that wasn't an option, she slunk down into her desk, trying to make herself as invisible as possible. Why couldn't there be a do-over button in life? After that ridiculous conversation, Caitlin was sure that Brie and her friends would never want anything to do with her.

The teacher wrote his name on the board. Mr. Hankins. After the principal, Mr. Eckhart, came on over the loudspeaker to welcome everyone, Mr. Hankins took attendance and explained that first period would be for catching up on homework, studying for any tests during the day, and free reading when everything else was finished.

Caitlin looked around the room and saw hundreds of books on racks and bookcases.

"Lots of books, huh?" the girl sitting on the other side of Caitlin whispered. She was a petite Asian girl with straight black hair and glasses.

"Yeah," Caitlin said.

"Do you like to read?" the girl asked.

What kind of question was that? "Yeah. Of course."

The girl smiled. "Me too."

"All right," Mr. Hankins said, "I need each of you to find a partner so we can go out in the hallway and get you your lockers. We have an even number of sixteen boys and twelve girls, so you shouldn't have any trouble finding someone. I know some of you are probably nervous about the whole locker business, but have no fear! We're going to practice opening your locker many times, after I pass out the combinations. You're sure to get the hang of it."

Caitlin looked over at the group of four girls. They were pointing and giggling, no doubt figuring out how to split their group into pairs. She didn't think she'd ever felt so jealous in her life.

"Hey." It was the girl on the other side of Caitlin. She turned and looked at her. "Do you want to be partners?"

Caitlin shrugged. "Okay."

"My name's Esther," she said.

"Hi," Caitlin said. "Nice to meet you."

"What's your name?" Esther asked.

Caitlin hadn't been giving Esther her full attention. She'd been trying to hear what the four girls were saying. It was too hard to hear though. "Oh, right. Sorry. It's Caitlin."

"Nice to meet you too, Caitlin."

Mr. Hankins came around and gave Esther and Caitlin a card with their locker number and combination on it. When Caitlin saw that it was locker number seventy-seven, she smiled as she thought about her Cabin 7 friends at camp. Maybe this was a good sign.

"What number did you get?" Caitlin asked Brie.

"Seventy-eight," she replied.

Caitlin's face lit up. "Oh good! We're right next to each other."

Brie gave her a little smile and returned to talking with her friends.

"Let's go," Mr. Hankins said. "Out into the hallway. Please keep your voices down, so we don't disturb the other classes."

Brie and her three friends stood up, and Caitlin watched as they walked to the front of the classroom. Even though the four girls were a variety of colors and shapes and sizes, they looked cute and happy, and Caitlin could tell they had fun together.

The fun girls. That's who they became in Caitlin's mind.

Caitlin knew what her mission was now. It was to get the fun girls to like her. Maybe she couldn't share a locker with one of them, but that didn't mean she couldn't hang out with them.

She could just see the five of them, painting each other's fingernails, talking about cute boys, and going to the movies together. They'd pass licorice and Junior Mints back and forth among one another like the best of friends do.

"Come on," Esther said as she stood up, pulling Caitlin back to reality. "Let's go."

With determination in her voice as she thought about finding a way in with those girls, Caitlin stood up, straight and tall. "Yep. I'm ready."

Caitlin didn't get a chance to talk to Brie again until dance class, right before lunch. Sixth graders were required to take some kind of physical education class, and the Beginning Dance class was one way to meet that requirement. The planning guide had said students would be exposed to ballet, tap, rhythm, and contemporary dance styles. Unlike lots of other girls, Caitlin had never taken dance classes, and she thought it sounded fun.

The girls changed in the locker room and then began to make their way to the dance studio, where they would meet up with any boys that were taking the class. Caitlin caught up with Brie and said, "Hi," as she stepped in line with her.

"Hey," Brie said.

"So, have you done much dancing?" Caitlin asked her.

"Yes," Brie said. "Why?"

"Just curious," Caitlin said. She started to tell her that this would be Caitlin's very first dance class, but she thought maybe she should keep that little bit of information to herself. She didn't want to say too much after the disastrous cheese conversation.

Once in the studio, the teacher, Ms. Sharp, talked for fifteen minutes or so about rules and expectations, just like every other teacher had on the first day. After that, they did some stretching.

"Since we don't have a lot of time today," Ms. Sharp said, "we'll wait and start our ballet unit on Wednesday. Today, I thought it'd be fun to put on some music and do some Zumba. The first day can be pretty stressful for some kids, so I thought we'd let loose a little and release some of that negative energy. Have any of you done Zumba before?"

About half the kids in the class raised their hands. Caitlin wasn't one of them.

"It's so much fun! You'll see. Just follow along as best you can. The important thing is to keep moving, get your groove on, and enjoy yourselves."

Ms. Sharp pressed the PLAY button on the CD player, and a hip-hop song came on. She raised her arms in the air and started shaking her hips, and Caitlin tried to follow along. Right, right, then left, left. Just as soon as she got the hang of one move, Ms. Sharp changed the routine and did something else. Caitlin tried to keep up, but she was always a step or two behind everyone.

Every once in a while, Caitlin looked over at Brie. It was like Brie had been doing Zumba her whole life. She could have been in a Zumba television commercial, that's how good she was. She made everything look easy. Effortless.

Caitlin tried harder.

"Here we go," Ms. Sharp said. "Time to shake those hips again."

They started the routine from the top. Caitlin shook her hips. Then she waved her arms in the air, right, right, then left, left.

I've got this. Caitlin thought. *Totally got this.*

Caitlin's movements got bigger and bolder. She caught Brie glancing over at her, so Caitlin smiled.

And still, she shook. And waved. And moved sideways, backward, and forward.

It was perfect, Caitlin thought. She and Brie would bond over Zumba. Surely this would be the beginning of a wonderful friendship. Maybe the two of them could even find a gym that offered Zumba classes, so they could go together on the weekends. Maybe they could get coffee afterward and hang out in a café.

Caitlin kept shaking and waving her arms as she envisioned her future as Brie's Zumba twin. When the music suddenly ended, it took Caitlin a few seconds to realize it was time to stop dancing. And then she realized something else.

She looked around the room and could see that everyone was watching her. Every. Single. Person. Some even had their hands over their mouths, trying to contain their laughter.

"That's enough," Ms. Sharp said. "One thing I will not tolerate is making fun of other students. Keep your eyes on me, and don't worry about what others are doing. Got it?"

"But how do we know whether someone's dancing or having a seizure?" some scrawny boy from the back called out. A bunch of kids laughed.

The teacher told the boy his comment was inappropriate and to go stand in the hallway. But it was Caitlin who wanted the solace of the hallway, so she took off, through the doors and out of that horrible room.

As she ran toward the locker room, blinking back the tears, she wondered if she would get in trouble for leaving class. Whatever. She didn't care. Her dancing days were over. As soon as the bell rang, she'd be going to see her counselor about taking something else besides dance class.

Anything else.

Chapter 9

Tulip
bright and cheery, like a good friend

Caitlin took the bus home after school, which dropped her off near Jade's house. She decided to see if Jade was home from school yet. She sent her mom a quick text to let her know she was stopping by her friend's house before she knocked on the door.

Seeing Jade's happy face after the terrible day Caitlin had was like seeing the first tulip after a long, cold winter.

"Surprise!" Caitlin sang out as Jade opened the door.

"Hey," Jade said with a smile. "This *is* a surprise. Come in!"

Caitlin stepped into the entryway, and Jade told her she could put her backpack and cardigan sweater on a little bench that sat there. The scent of chocolate hung in the air. Caitlin's stomach growled. She'd hardly eaten any of her lunch, since she'd spent most of her lunch period talking to her counselor about changing classes.

"Wow, cute belt," Jade said after Caitlin took off her sweater. "Is that new?"

Caitlin sighed. "Well, I'm glad someone likes it. My mom and I made it last night. I thought it was the coolest thing ever, and for some reason, I thought it would have magical powers and make me all kinds of friends today."

"But it didn't?"

Caitlin shook her head.

"Come on. Let's go to the kitchen. My mom made brownies."

"Hi, Caitlin," Jade's mom said. "Nice to see you." She looked at Jade. "I have some paperwork to do, so I'll be in the den."

After Jade's mom left, the girls grabbed some brownies and poured glasses of milk before sitting on stools at the kitchen counter.

Caitlin took a bite of her brownie that was still slightly warm, which made it a little bit gooey, just the way she liked it. "Mmm," she said. "So good. At least I did one thing right today. Stopped by to see you."

"Why do I get the feeling things didn't go very well at the new school?" Jade asked.

Caitlin laughed. "Because they didn't. At all!"

She took a drink of milk and then she told her friend everything. She told her about the fun girls and the ridiculous cheese conversation. After that, she told her about the dance class and the mean seizure comment. And then she told her about spending most of her lunch period in the counselor's office.

Jade listened intently, only averting her eyes every once in a while to take a bite of brownie.

After Caitlin finished talking, she sat back and sighed. "I just really wanted Brie and her group of friends to like me, you know? They seemed like the type of girls I belong with."

Jade finished her milk and set the empty glass down. "You could tell that just by looking at them?"

"I know it sounds weird, but yes. I could see us doing crafts or going to the movies together. They looked . . . fun!"

"You know what you have to do?" Jade asked as she stood up and took the empty plates and glasses to the sink.

"What?" Caitlin asked.

Jade came back to the counter. "You have to get involved in things. That's the best way to make friends. Once this first week is over, they'll start announcing activities. Sports. Clubs. The fall play. That kind of thing."

"Yeah," Caitlin said. "I definitely want to try out for the play. Theater is one of the reasons I wanted to go to this school. You can forget about sports though. Not really my thing."

"Well, as long as you get involved in something," Jade said. "I'm thinking of trying out for volleyball this year. Who knows if I'll be any good, but I think it looks like fun."

Caitlin suddenly realized she hadn't been a very good friend. This had been Jade's first day at a new school too. Of course, a lot of kids they went to school with last year were going to Jade's middle school, but still, it wasn't very nice to not ask about it.

"I'm sorry," Caitlin told her friend. "All I've done is talk about my horrible day. How'd your first day go?"

"It was fine. Melanie Booker is my locker partner. We have a bunch of classes together. Oh my gosh, our PE teacher is so funny. He *sang* to us while we ran laps around the gym." She started to sing, " 'You are never, ever, ever going to stop the running.' " She laughed. "It was hysterical. Whatever song he could think of, he sang and then turned it into a crazy health and fitness song."

Caitlin tried to smile. She also tried to push down the regret that was rising up, telling her she shouldn't have applied to ACMA. She could have been having a good time with Jade in that PE class.

"Come on," Jade said. "Let's go to my room. My mom bought me a bunch of new beads. We can make bracelets or something."

"Ooh, that sounds like fun," Caitlin said as she hopped up. She pulled her phone out of her pocket and looked at the time. Her mom had texted her back, asking her to be home by four thirty. "I have to go in thirty minutes though."

"No problem," Jade said.

If only the rest of the day had been this easy, Caitlin thought.

Later, when Caitlin got home, she was surprised to find her dad's car in the driveway. Usually he didn't get home until at least six o'clock.

Her first and only thought was that he'd been fired.

The butterflies she'd felt all day at school came back with a vengeance. She considered turning around and going back to Jade's house, where things were normal. But of course she couldn't stay there forever. She'd have to come home sometime.

Caitlin opened the door quietly and listened. What she

was listening for, she wasn't sure. Yelling? Tears? Telephone calls to family members breaking the terrible news?

She could hear muffled voices upstairs, so that's where she headed. She stopped outside of her parents' room, where the doors were slightly ajar, and listened.

"Miranda, how many times do I have to tell you, I don't know," her dad said. "I don't know when they'll make the decision about my position. Or any of the other positions, for that matter."

"But it's not fair," her mom said. "It's not fair to keep us guessing and wondering like this. How are we supposed to live in the meantime?"

"Just like we talked about. We only buy the absolute essentials right now, and we save money like it's going out of style. We have to be ready, just in case."

"I'm trying, but it's hard," her mom said. Caitlin thought it sounded like her mom might start crying. "I canceled the satellite TV, like you told me. The kids are going to be pretty unhappy with us."

"What about the girls' phones?" Mr. Rogers said. "We'd save a lot of money if we canceled those."

"Don, isn't that a little extreme? If you lose your job and go on unemployment benefits, then, yes, I'll cancel

76

the phones. But that's how I stay in touch with them. I don't want them to be without phones unless it's absolutely necessary."

Caitlin didn't want to hear anymore. It was so depressing. She tiptoed down the hall, toward her room.

"Hey, Peaches," her dad said.

Caitlin turned around. "Oh. Hi."

"Glad to see you're home. How was your first day?"

Caitlin didn't want to add to her parents' problems. "It was fine," she replied quickly. "How come you're home so early?"

"Oh, I had a dentist appointment, so I took the afternoon off. My teeth are all clean and shiny, see?" He gave her a big grin.

"Very nice."

Caitlin's mom came out into the hallway. "Honey, it's your turn to help me with dinner. Put your things away, wash up, and then come down, all right?"

"Okay. I'll be there in a few minutes."

As Caitlin washed her hands in the bathroom, she looked at herself in the mirror. She wasn't sure what was worse, making a fool of herself at school or hearing her parents argue about money. At least at school she had the opportunity to make things better. There wasn't anything she could do to help her parents with their finances.

Caitlin decided Jade was right. She had to find ways to get involved in things at school. Not only would it help her to make some friends, but it would also give her something to keep her mind off her parents' problems. She had a feeling home wasn't going to be a very fun place to be for a while. Especially with no satellite TV.

It was up to her to try and make her own fun.

Chapter 10

Aster
a favorite of butterflies

The rest of the week was fairly uneventful. Caitlin had decided to keep her head down and try to be invisible, so people would hopefully forget about her embarrassing first day.

At lunchtime, she sat at the "reading table," set up specifically for students who didn't want to talk while eating lunch but wanted to read instead. Of course, it wasn't that Caitlin didn't *want* to talk to people, she just didn't really have anyone to talk to.

Every day, she watched Brie and her three friends having the time of their lives at their table. Two of them bought hot lunch every day, while the other two brought sack lunches from home. Sometimes one of the girls who brought a lunch from home brought treats for all of the girls, like little candy bars or a big bag of grapes to share. It seemed like something Caitlin, Mia, Libby, and Hannah would have done if they were lucky enough to go to the same school.

When a letter from Libby arrived on Thursday, Caitlin was thrilled. She made herself wait to open it, however, and took it to school to read during lunch on Friday. She told herself it would be good to have something to look forward to. And it was. She sat down in her usual spot, took out her ham and cheese sandwich, and carefully opened the letter from Libby.

Dear Caitlin,

Hello! How are you? I hope this letter finds you well. I've only been home a few days now and am missing you and the other girls something fierce. I thought I'd write to you first, since you and I seemed to be the most nervous about the new school year.

I hope things are going splendidly. By the time you get this (since it has to fly over an ocean to reach you), both of us will be back at school. My new secondary school is called Bennett Memorial. I'm wondering what it's going to be like, being in a school with sixteen-year-olds. The way you do it there in America, with the older teens in high school and the younger teens in middle school, sounds much better to me.

Did you come home from camp to find any surprises? I certainly did. My best friend, Rebecca, has taken up with a new group of friends. They'll all be going to a different secondary school than me, so Rebecca hasn't wanted to include me. I've felt fairly left out since I arrived home. She seems to be crazy for one of the boys in the group, and he's all she wants to talk about. It's so annoying! Why must girls be like that, all because of a cute boy? It doesn't make any sense to me.

In other news, Dexter was so happy to see me. I think he missed me as much as I missed him. We've been going on lots of walks together, since my best friend is too busy for me.

Please write back when you can. I miss you!
Your Cabin 7 BFF,
Libby

Caitlin smiled as she folded up the letter and put it back in the envelope. Libby was so formal in the way she talked sometimes, and now Caitlin could see she wrote her letters that way too. Sweet and proper Libby. Oh, how Caitlin missed her. And the rest of her camp friends.

A teacher came to the reading table carrying yellow and blue flyers. He passed out one of each to every student. Caitlin opened the blue one first and read it.

INTERESTED IN GOVERNMENT?

DO YOU HAVE WHAT IT TAKES TO BE A LEADER?

STUDENT COUNCIL BOARD MEMBERS

AND CLASS PRESIDENT ELECTIONS

COMING SOON!

STUDENT LEADERS MEET WITH SCHOOL ADMINISTRATORS

TO DISCUSS STUDENT PERSPECTIVES. THEY ALSO

PROMOTE STUDENT VOLUNTEERING AND DECIDE ON

FUND-RAISING EFFORTS.

FILL OUT THE FORM BELOW AND SUBMIT IT ALONG WITH A

STATEMENT OF NO MORE THAN ONE HUNDRED WORDS ABOUT

WHY YOU ARE INTERESTED IN RUNNING FOR A POSITION.

A GROUP OF TEACHERS WILL SELECT THE STUDENT

NOMINEES BASED ON THE WRITTEN STATEMENTS.
THE NOMINEES WILL BE RESPONSIBLE FOR PUTTING
TOGETHER CAMPAIGNS AND GIVING A
THREE-MINUTE SPEECH.

READY, SET, RUN FOR STUDENT GOVERNMENT!

The yellow flyer said:

ANNOUNCING THE FALL PLAY

CHARLOTTE'S WEB: A MUSICAL
INSPIRED BY THE BOOK WRITTEN BY E. B. WHITE
DIRECTED BY MRS. SEARS

AUDITION SIGN-UP SHEET IS OUTSIDE THE
MUSIC ROOM.

A play based on *Charlotte's Web*. Caitlin felt like it was a sign, after meeting Sonny and Wilbur last week. She was meant to try out for this play, and something told her she would get a part. A really good part.

As for student government, there was one position that

interested her above anything else. President of the sixth grade. Because, she figured, if she could somehow manage to become president, Brie and her friends wouldn't be able to resist including her in their group. Hopefully they'd stop seeing her as a bothersome bumblebee and more like a graceful and friendly butterfly.

Caitlin stuffed the fliers and the letter into her backpack and then threw away her trash, wanting to get to the music room before the warning bell rang.

"Hey, Caitlin."

She turned around to find Esther standing there.

"Oh. Hi."

"I wanted to tell you, I'm forming a Battle of the Books team, so we'll be ready when the books are announced in November. I know you said you like to read. Would you want to be on my team?"

"Battle of the Books? What's that?" Caitlin asked.

Esther tucked her hair behind her ear. "There's a list of books and each team assigns members to read a bunch of them. Teams compete against each other, answering trivia questions about the books. It's really fun, and there are prizes awarded at the championship battle."

Caitlin looked at the clock on the wall. The bell was due

to ring in just a few minutes. She really wanted to get her name on that list for the *Charlotte's Web* auditions.

"Yeah, okay," she told Esther. "I can be on your team, I guess. I gotta run. See ya later!"

Esther smiled. "Okay, thank you! I'll let you know when our first team meeting is."

Caitlin waved and hurried off toward the music room. As she made her way past the table where Brie and her friends sat, she heard someone say, "Come on. Let's go to the music room before the bell rings."

She couldn't believe it. This was *really* her lucky day. The fun girls were trying out for the musical too! This was perfect. After all, nothing said friendship more than the story of Charlotte and Wilbur.

With all of the excitement going on, Caitlin wasn't paying very close attention. One of the girls at Brie's table had her leg sticking out just slightly, and Caitlin didn't see it. She tripped on the girl's foot and landed flat on the floor, sprawled out on her stomach. Completely embarrassed, Caitlin popped up just as quickly as she'd fallen down. Everything hurt, but she told herself to ignore the pain, along with the snickers and whispers going on around her.

Just get out of here, she told herself. *Fast.*

"Are you okay?" she heard Esther ask from behind her.

But Caitlin didn't give her an answer. She rushed out of the room, once again hoping to escape the humiliation that didn't seem to want to leave her alone.

So much for being a graceful butterfly.

Chapter 11

Calla Lily
not embarrassed to be fragrance free

"*I*saac?" Caitlin called out as she opened his bedroom door.

Caitlin looked around his room and cringed. Apparently their mother hadn't been in there in a while. It was like a giant LEGO monster had vomited plastic blocks everywhere. On his nightstand. In his laundry basket. All over his unmade bed. She found herself wondering if he just crawled in and slept there with them. *Ouch.*

"Isaac, I know you're in here somewhere," she said. "Come on, we have to get ready to go to the soup kitchen. They had a couple of volunteers call in sick, so we're helping out tonight."

"I'm in here."

His little, muffled voice came from the closet. She went

over and opened the door. A giant green and brown afghan their grandmother had made hung like a curtain from the clothes rack, held there with the help of some duct tape (lots and lots of duct tape).

"What are you doing in there?" Caitlin asked her brother.

"Hiding from zombies."

"Oh. So zombies don't like afghans? I'll have to remember that. Look, I don't want to mess up your fort or whatever it is that you've built, so can you come out here?"

"Is it safe?"

"I promise, there are no zombies in this room. Or even in this house."

"What if they plan a sneak attack?"

Caitlin pinched her lips together to keep from laughing. "I will protect you. I'm very strong, you know."

He poked his head out. "No. You're not."

"Just . . . come out here." Caitlin watched as he stepped out and carefully shut the door. "Are you all right?"

"I'm scared."

"Of what?"

He shrugged. "Of zombies. And maybe everything."

She knelt down and pulled him into a hug. "It's okay. There's really nothing to be afraid of."

He held her tightly for a moment before he pulled away and said, "Maybe we should all get jobs where they pay us instead of working at the soup kitchen for free."

"Are you worried about money?"

"Yes," he said. "Mom and Dad are too. Caitlin, they got rid of all the good TV channels!"

"I know. Sorry about that."

"Caitlin! Isaac! Come on, we have to go!" It was their mom, yelling from downstairs.

Caitlin ushered her brother into the hallway and then to the bathroom. "I'll wait right here for you," she said. "Make sure you comb your hair while you're in there."

A few minutes later, they were in their van and on the way.

"How come Jessi isn't coming?" Caitlin asked.

"She had other plans," her mom replied.

"Plans? Like what?" It didn't seem fair to Caitlin that Jessi didn't have to go with them.

"She's studying with a friend. For a test on Monday."

Caitlin rolled her eyes. Studying on a Friday night? Right. And money grows on trees, so they shouldn't be worried about Dad's job after all.

When they got to the kitchen, Mrs. Watson was there to

greet them again. She wore the same apron and the same button as last time. Caitlin wondered if that was like her soup kitchen uniform.

Mrs. Watson put the three of them to work washing and cutting up celery and carrots. Caitlin and Isaac washed, while their mom used the very large, very sharp knife.

When it was time to serve, Caitlin was given the task of handing out vegetables. Isaac got to hand out the cookies.

"Yes!" Isaac said with a fist pump, as if he had just been told he got to eat all the cookies rather than simply hand them out.

Caitlin recognized some of the people from last time, but others she hadn't seen before. There was even a girl who had been in her dance class that first day at school. Caitlin remembered her because the girl wore her hair super-short, something Caitlin could never pull off. But this girl had big, round eyes, beautiful skin, and prominent cheekbones, so it totally worked on her. As Caitlin thought back to that embarrassing class, she wished she could run and hide. Would the girl remember her? Would she mention the class at all? Caitlin found herself hoping she didn't say a thing — just took her food and kept going down the line. But no such luck.

"Hi," the girl said as Caitlin put carrots and celery sticks on her plate. "You go to ACMA, right?"

"Yeah," Caitlin replied.

"I felt really bad for you in dance class that day. It was mean, what that boy said. I didn't think there was anything wrong with your dancing."

"Oh. Well, thanks."

"Move along, Tezra," said the woman beside her. "You're holding up the line."

"Hang on, Mom." Tezra leaned in and whispered to Caitlin, "Don't tell anyone you saw me here, 'kay? Please? We're just going through a rough time right now. Need a little help, you know? We only come a couple of times a week."

"No worries," Caitlin replied. "I won't say a thing."

"Thanks," Tezra said. Her brown eyes were warm. Kind.

Caitlin watched as Tezra and her mom went and sat down. And here Caitlin had been worried about Tezra seeing her because of the stupid dance class, never thinking about what it must be like for Tezra. Of course Tezra must be feeling kind of embarrassed about being seen here. But she didn't need to worry. Caitlin would never judge her. After all, it wasn't Tezra's fault they were having a hard time financially.

Sonny interrupted Caitlin's thoughts as he came through the line. "Well look who's here, Wilbur. Caitlin and Isaac. Nice to see you two again."

Wilbur poked his tiny head out of Sonny's jacket, just like last time.

"Can we come pet him again when we're finished serving?" Isaac asked.

"Of course you can," Sonny replied.

"I'm trying out for the musical at school," Caitlin told him. "It made me think of you, because we're doing *Charlotte's Web*."

Sonny grinned. "Is that right? Well, you know what? Depending on how much tickets cost, I sure would love to come and watch that play. Will you let me know all the details when you have them?"

"Sure," Caitlin said.

"Why, the last time I saw a play was when I worked at that elementary school. Every year the first graders put on a production of *The Little Red Hen*. Cutest thing you ever did see, that's for sure." Sonny looked at Isaac. "See you at my table pretty soon."

"Okay," Isaac said.

"Can I have two of those?" Sonny asked, pointing at the cookies.

Isaac nodded and put another cookie on his plate. "You gonna give one to Wilbur?" Isaac asked.

Sonny shook his head. "Nope. I'm gonna save both of them for the two of you, since you'll be hungry after all your hard work. Right?"

"Right!" Isaac said.

After Sonny left, Isaac turned to Caitlin and said, "I like Sonny and Wilbur. They're nice."

Caitlin almost didn't hear her brother, as she'd been distracted, watching Mrs. Watson, who had sat down across from Tezra and her mom. It looked like they were having a pretty intense conversation. Mrs. Watson was doing a lot of nodding, most likely being a friendly ear, just like her button said.

"Caitlin?" Isaac said. "Did you hear me? There's a lot of nice people here, huh? That girl from your school seems nice too."

"Yeah," Caitlin said. "I guess so."

"You gonna be friends with her?" Isaac asked.

Caitlin was embarrassed about the dance class. Tezra was embarrassed about being seen at the soup kitchen. If they ran into each other Monday, would either of them even admit to having met each other?

Caitlin's guess was probably not.

"I don't think so," Caitlin said quietly. "I mean, she doesn't even know my name."

Chapter 12

Rose
Smells like happiness

The following week, on Thursday, after school, Caitlin wandered around their local flower shop, Flowerworks, while her mom placed an order for a small bouquet for a friend who was in the hospital. Tucked away in the refrigerated cases, behind glass doors, were buckets of loose flowers, like roses and lilies. There were also lots of pretty arrangements, ready to be picked up and taken home or given to a friend.

Caitlin loved everything about the flower shop. How it was so colorful and cheerful. How people came here to send good wishes for a special occasion or to make someone feel better. And most of all, how it all seemed to smell like . . . love.

She walked over and stood by her mom at the counter.

"How are you doing, Caitlin?" Trudy, the owner, asked her. She insisted on being called by her first name. "School going okay?"

"Yes, thank you."

Caitlin's mom put her arm around her daughter. "She found out today that she's been selected to run for class president. Isn't that exciting?"

Trudy smiled. "That *is* exciting! Do you have your slogan yet?"

Caitlin gave her a curious look. "Slogan? What do you mean?"

"Well, when I was in school, kids would come up with these catchy sayings, usually around their names. You know, something like: Vote for Dan, he's our man."

"Does it have to rhyme?" Caitlin asked. "Because if it does, I think I'm in trouble."

Both Trudy and her mom laughed. "No, it doesn't have to rhyme," her mom replied. "I think when your sister ran in the eighth grade, her slogan was: If you must waste your vote on someone, waste it on Jessi."

"So it should be funny," Caitlin said. She grimaced. "This is gonna be hard!"

"Maybe your sister will help you."

"And maybe Trudy will let me take all these flowers home," Caitlin joked. "I don't think so."

Trudy walked out from behind the counter and went to the glass case. She opened the door and took out a yellow rose. "I can't let you take all of them home, but I can certainly let you take this one."

Caitlin smiled. "Aw, thank you so much." She took a sniff, savoring the sweet and familiar scent.

"You're welcome," Trudy said. "And good luck. I hope you win."

All the way home, Caitlin thought about a slogan. She couldn't get the idea of trying to rhyme out of her head.

Don't be a pumpkin, vote for Caitlin.

Voting for Caitlin is truly a win-win.

She's got a great grin, vote for Caitlin.

She shook her head, trying to erase her horrible ideas. It had to be unique. Funny. And most of all, catchy.

"You know what else you need to do," her mom said, saving Caitlin from thinking of any more bad slogans, "is to think of things you might do when you get elected."

"What kind of things?"

"You know, suggesting new clubs. Or coming up with new policies. When I was in school, taking on the cafeteria menu was always a big issue. I remember this one kid, Gerald, promised to get rid of the meat loaf if he was elected."

"Gross. You had meat loaf at school?"

"Yeah. Kids called it the mystery meat, because no one was sure what was in it."

Caitlin shuddered. "We don't have anything horrible like meat loaf. But maybe I can think of a fun new club to offer up." Her mind started spinning. "Maybe a jewelry club, where we could make jewelry."

"How about making it a bit broader, and that could just be one activity you do?" her mom suggested.

"So, what, call it a fun activity club?"

Her mom shrugged. "What about a friendship club? Do they have anything like that?"

"Oh my gosh, Mom, that is perfect. I love it!"

She looked at Caitlin. "What? You actually like something your mother suggested? Well, get the record book out and write that down. Because I'm guessing that won't happen again for another ten years."

Caitlin laughed as they pulled into the driveway of Isaac's friend's house to pick him up. When Isaac jumped into the van a minute later, he was all smiles. Caitlin thought about how much better it was to see her brother like that rather than all scared, hiding in his closet.

"You have fun playing?" Caitlin asked him, as she turned around from the front seat.

"We played *Spacegators*."

"What's that?" Caitlin asked.

"A really cool video game that takes place on another planet. And there are all kinds of strange creatures you have to stay away from, called spacegators."

"It's not too scary?" their mom asked.

"Nope. It's fun. Like Zach's older brother says, 'Fun is the name of the game, Mom.'"

"Hey, maybe that would be a good slogan," Caitlin said. "Vote for Caitlin, because fun is the name of the game."

"Ooh, I like it," her mom said. "It goes well with the friendship club, right?"

"It's not really funny though," Caitlin said. "Maybe I need to get more creative. I wish I knew a comedian. How come we don't have any comedians in our family?"

"I'm a comedian," Isaac said. "Want to hear a joke?"

"You bet," their mom said. "Give it to us, little man."

"Why don't skeletons fight each other?" Isaac asked.

"I don't know," Caitlin said. "Why don't skeletons fight each other?"

"Because they don't have the guts!" Isaac said before he let out a loud but adorable laugh.

Caitlin and her mom both laughed too, though Caitlin knew it was more because they loved Isaac's laugh than his silly jokes.

"Think you can put that in your slogan, honey?" her mom asked.

"I could, I guess, but I'm pretty sure you have to be an eight-year-old boy to really appreciate that one," Caitlin said.

When they got home, Caitlin jumped out of the van with her rose and got the mail. She squealed when she saw a letter from Hannah.

"Here," she said as she practically threw the rest of the mail at her mom. "I'm going to my room."

"Better put that rose in some water," her mom called out as Caitlin rushed through the front door.

Caitlin went to the kitchen and got a vase of water for the rose, like her mom had suggested, and carried it up to the room. She put the rose next to her bed, and then she opened the envelope.

Dear Caitlin,

Hey there! How's it going? How's the new school? I've been thinking about you, hoping things are going okay. The letter you wrote the night before your first day made it sound like you were about as nervous as a mouse in a barn full of cats. You're so nice, I'm sure you've made friends by now. Do they have any clubs you can join? I'm in a club here at my school, and it's a lot of fun.

I've worn the headband you made me quite a few times since I've been home. It's so cute, and I've gotten a lot of compliments on it. How's the bracelet? Is it bringing you lots of luck? I can't wait to see what charms everyone picks out.

I've heard from you and Libby, but nothing from Mia yet. Hope everything is all right in her neck of the woods. Or, you know, her bay of the ocean.

Here's something funny. While I was away at camp, my mom and grandma canned applesauce, tomato sauce, strawberry jam, and some other things I can't think of right now. Guess how many jars. Go on. Guess.

50? Nope.

100? Nope.

207 jars. Yes, I counted. I know, I'm weird. But they were on shelves in the basement and I

couldn't believe how many there were, and then I had to know exactly how many.

I'm pretty sure I'll be having applesauce and spaghetti every night for the rest of the year until I go back to camp again. Speaking of camp, when I told my parents how much fun I had, they were like, "Told you so!" Don't you hate it when our parents are right for a change?

Okay, gotta run. Time for supper. Guess what we're having? You'll never guess. (I'm kidding — you totally will.)

Your Cabin 7 BFF,
Hannah

If only Caitlin could call Hannah, she thought. Hannah would be able to come up with a brilliant slogan — something unique and funny. She thought about writing a letter and asking Hannah to think of some suggestions, but there wasn't time. Caitlin needed to make posters over the weekend and work on her campaign speech for the assembly that was scheduled for next Thursday.

Unless she could think of something better in the next twenty-four hours, fun would be the name of the game for Caitlin and her campaign.

Fun wasn't a bad way to go really. Who wouldn't like the idea of having more fun at school? The fun girls might finally notice her and realize Caitlin would be an awesome addition to their little group.

That's what she was hoping for anyway.

Chapter 13

Daisy
a real winner

Friday morning, in first period, Caitlin sat down next to Brie. The fun girls were talking about going to see a movie together Saturday night.

"Let's go out to eat first," Brie said. "Where should we go?"

"What about that new Mexican restaurant? I've heard they have amazing taco salads."

"No, let's go out for pizza. Maybe Brandon will be working. Seeing Brandon is way better than having an amazing taco salad, right?"

All the girls sighed. "Brandon," Brie said. "I just can't even . . . no guy should be allowed to be that cute."

One said, "Last time I was there, with my family, I went back to the counter so many times, it wasn't even funny. I'd ask for extra napkins or more Parmesan, until I couldn't think of anything else to ask for."

All of the girls giggled.

They carried on about Brandon for another minute until, finally, there was a pause in their conversation. Caitlin tapped Brie on the elbow.

"Hi," Caitlin said, smiling. "Hey, can I ask you something?"

Brie shrugged. "Sure."

"You know I was chosen to run for class president, right? I'm thinking about focusing my campaign around having more fun at school. What do you think of the idea of having a friendship club here?"

Brie's eyes narrowed, like she was really thinking about it. "A friendship club. Wow. That sounds . . . cute."

"Do you think people would go for it? I mean, would you and your friends be interested in something like that?"

"Maybe. If the activities in the club were actually fun, you know?"

"Oh yeah," Caitlin said. "I'd work hard to make sure they are."

The bell rang.

"Thanks," Caitlin whispered to Brie. "Thanks for your help."

After a few quick announcements from the principal over the loudspeaker, Mr. Hankins stood up to take roll.

Caitlin was so happy, she could hardly sit still. Brie liked her idea. With the invention of the friendship club, Caitlin would finally have a way to get to know the four girls and become part of their group. This was all working out perfectly.

She opened her notebook and started writing. It was time to work on the greatest speech ever written. A speech about all the ways she would make school more fun.

While the class worked quietly at their desks, Esther passed Caitlin a note.

Hi Caitlin,

First Battle of the Books meeting will be next Thursday, after school, in the library. I want to introduce all the members to each other and give us a chance to get to know each other a little bit. Bring a favorite book along, if you'd like. It's always fun to talk about books, right? My mom will be happy to give you a ride home after the meeting.

Esther

Caitlin stuffed the note into her backpack and went back to her notebook. She'd have to worry about the Battle of the Books later. She had a campaign to plan.

*   *   *

On Saturday, Jade came over to help Caitlin make posters. Mrs. Rogers had gone to the craft store and bought a bunch of poster board, markers, big smiley face stickers, and balloons. If her campaign was about fun, Caitlin had to make sure her posters looked fun.

The girls carried the supplies up to Caitlin's room and shut the door.

"Pretty rose," Jade said as she set the stuff on Caitlin's bed. Jade went over and took a whiff. "Mmm. Smells so good. Maybe fresh flowers should be a part of your campaign."

"What do you mean?" Caitlin asked, taking a poster board and placing it on the floor.

"Pass out flowers to everyone and ask them to vote for you."

"That would get expensive," Caitlin said.

"Not if we picked daisies from the field across from my house. Wouldn't cost you anything."

Caitlin bounced up. "Oh my gosh! That's kind of a genius idea. Are there a lot of them? Daisies, I mean?"

"Oh yeah. I can help you pick some if you want me to."

"So I just put them in a basket and walk around and ask people to vote for me?"

Jade shrugged. "Yeah. Why not? It's better than stupid buttons, which you would have to pay for and hardly anyone would wear, right?"

"I think you're right. Do you think daisies are fun?" Caitlin wanted to make sure everything tied in with her theme.

"I think so," Jade said. "Kids make daisy chains out of the tiny daisies, right? That's pretty fun, if you ask me."

Caitlin gave her friend a hug. "Thank you. I can't believe how everything is coming together so well. This is going to be the best campaign ever."

Jade pointed to the pile of posters. "If we don't pass out from making all these posters."

"My mom made us cupcakes," Caitlin said. "Does that help?"

Jade wiggled her eyebrows. "What flavor?"

"Only your favorite. Red velvet."

Jade jumped off the bed, grabbed a poster and some markers, and threw herself on the floor. "Come on, girl. What are you doing, wasting time talking? We need to get these posters made. Snap to it, as my mother likes to say."

Caitlin laughed. "Hey, maybe I should pass out cupcakes instead of daisies."

"That's crazy," Jade said. "Too much work."

"You just want all the cupcakes for yourself," Caitlin said.

"Bwahahaha." Jade gave an evil laugh. "You know me too well."

Chapter 14

Hydrangea
a unique choice for weddings

On Monday morning, Mrs. Rogers drove Caitlin to school with all of her campaign stuff. They got there thirty minutes early, to give Caitlin plenty of time before school started. Once inside, she went to work hanging her posters in the hallway. Ten was the limit, and she and Jade had worked really hard to make them fun and colorful. They'd taped balloons on the two corners and put smiley face stickers all over them.

As Caitlin hung her posters, she noticed the ones made by her two opponents, Della and Kristopher.

Markers: Five Bucks
Posters: Ten Bucks
Della as Sixth-Grade Class President: Priceless.

Forget Obi-Wan Kenobi
Vote for Kristopher
for Sixth-Grade Class President
He's our only hope!

Butterflies swarmed Caitlin's stomach. They'd found some funny slogans. Creative and unique. Hers wasn't anything special. It was almost boring compared to theirs.

Vote for Caitlin
for Sixth-Grade Class President,
because fun is the name of the game!

She told herself there wasn't anything she could do now but hope for the best. Once all of her posters were hung, Caitlin picked up the basket of daisies and made her way toward the front of the school. She'd kept them in a vase of water overnight and then piled them into a cute basket her mom had found. It reminded her of the time she'd been the flower girl for her aunt's wedding when she was five years old, except then, she'd carried a small basket of pale blue hydrangeas.

As kids began coming into school, Caitlin started handing out the daisies.

"Hi, I'm Caitlin, and I'm running for class president."

The first few girls took the daisies and said, "Thanks."

When she tried to hand it to a boy, he said, "No way. What am I going to do with a stupid flower?"

"Uh . . ." Caitlin tried to think of a response, but the boy kept walking.

Caitlin turned around and tried to hand some to a group of boys. "Are you serious?" one of them asked her.

She took a deep breath and told herself not to let it bother her. All of the boys would probably vote for Kristopher anyway.

Stick to the girls, she told herself.

And that's exactly what she did. It only took about ten minutes, and then her daisies were gone. She looked at the empty basket in satisfaction before she made her way toward the sixth-grade hallway and her locker.

When she turned the corner, the hallway was so crowded, she could hardly make her way through.

"What's going on?" she asked someone.

"Look what Della is handing out," a girl said, shoving a baggie of something in front of Caitlin. Caitlin reached out and moved the girl's hand back so she could see what was inside. It was a sugar cookie, frosted with the words *Vote for Della.*

"Wow," Caitlin said, kicking herself for not making cupcakes to pass out like she'd suggested to Jade.

"I know, right?" the girl said before she moved along.

Caitlin looked around to see if any of the girls were talking about the flowers she'd handed out. She looked and looked for any sign of a flower. The only one she could find was a poor trampled daisy on the ground.

Why didn't she see more of them? she wondered.

And that's when it hit her. She'd passed out flowers to people coming through the front door, not knowing if they were sixth, seventh, or eighth graders. She should have been passing them out here, in the sixth-grade hallway, like Della had done. These were the students who would be voting. These were the people who really mattered.

As Caitlin made her way toward her locker, she got caught in a mob of kids trying to get something that Kristopher was handing out. Caitlin stood on her tippy-toes, wanting to see what it was, but she couldn't get a good look. Whatever it was, everyone seemed to want one, which meant it most definitely wasn't a flower.

When Caitlin reached her locker, Esther was there, a baggie of cookies in one hand and a baggie of something else in the other.

"I guess they both decided the way to the voter's heart is through the stomach," Esther said.

"Can I see what Kristopher made?" Caitlin asked.

"Sure."

Inside the baggie were what appeared to be five teensy-tiny red and blue lightsabers.

"What are they made out of?" Caitlin asked.

Esther pointed to a label attached to the baggie.

" 'Remember, Kristopher is your only hope. In the meantime, enjoy these lightsabers made out of pretzels and Fruit Roll-Ups. May the force to vote be with you.' "

Caitlin leaned her head against the locker and closed her eyes. "This is not good," she groaned.

"Did you forget to bring something?" Esther asked her.

Caitlin turned around and looked at Esther. "I brought daisies. I'd offer to give you one, but I already passed them out to a bunch of seventh and eighth graders."

Esther gave her a funny look. "Why'd you do that?"

"I didn't mean to. I thought passing them out by the front doors was the way to go. But after they were gone, and I came here, I realized this was the perfect place." Caitlin shook her head. "What a waste."

"You could try again tomorrow," Esther said.

"We practically picked the field clean though," Caitlin said.

"Oh," Esther said. "I'm sorry. Do you want me to help you think of something else to do?"

Caitlin looked at the clever posters that hung across the hallway. And then she looked at the snacks Della and Kristopher had made that had impressed everyone.

"Thanks," Caitlin said, turning to open her locker, "but it may be too late. I don't want to look like I'm copying them, showing up with some kind of clever homemade treat."

"Then don't make something," Esther said. "If your focus is on fun, what if you passed out fun-size candy bars?"

At the word *fun-size*, Caitlin spun around and looked at Esther again, her eyes big and round. "Oh my gosh. That is a fantastic idea!" She remembered watching the fun girls eat the fun-size candy bars one of them had brought along at lunchtime to share. "Who doesn't like candy, right?"

Esther smiled. Caitlin noticed she had braces on her top teeth. How come she hadn't noticed that before?

Caitlin got her books out of their locker and stepped aside. "Thanks, Esther. I feel so much better. I can still do something that will make people remember me. Tonight I'll go to the store and buy a bunch of bags of candy bars . . ."

And then she stopped. Because if she wanted to pass out the candy bars, she'd have to come up with the money to buy them. And she didn't have any money.

Chapter 15

Snowdrop
a pretty winter flower

All day, Caitlin thought about what she might do to get her mom to agree to buy bags of candy for her campaign. Her mom had made it pretty clear to Caitlin after shopping at the craft store for the poster supplies that she didn't want to spend any more money on the project. She'd told Caitlin that part of being a good leader was coming up with creative solutions to problems, and sometimes that meant creative solutions to money problems.

"But people who run for President of the United States spend a lot of money on their campaigns, Mom," Caitlin had told her. "We talked about that in Social Studies."

"Yes, but you're not running for President of the United States," her mom had replied. She'd patted Caitlin on her back and said, "Now if you decide to do that in about twenty-five years, by all means, come and see me. I'll give you a big, fat donation, okay?"

Now, as the final bell rang, Caitlin had one last thing to do before she got to go home after a long, disappointing day: audition for the school play.

She made her way toward the auditorium, wondering if something might finally go her way. She really wanted the part of Charlotte. At home, Caitlin and her mom had watched videos online of performances of the play at other schools. One performance she'd watched featured Charlotte in this amazing costume so that every time the girl playing the spider moved her arms, all of the spider's legs moved, alongside the girl's body. Her mom had said they must have been attached with thread or wire or something.

Caitlin took a seat toward the back of the auditorium and sunk down, trying to be invisible for now. Each student had been assigned a time to try out. Caitlin's turn was in about ten minutes. She felt butterflies in her stomach again, though this time, they felt more like angry bees.

Just as Caitlin had settled down into her seat, the fun girls walked into the auditorium. One of the girls went all the way toward the front and stood there, waiting. The other three girls took a seat in the row in front of Caitlin.

"She's going to do great," Caitlin overheard Brie say. "As long as she doesn't get too nervous, the part of Charlotte will be hers."

"And hopefully the part of Wilbur is yours, right, Brie?" one of the other girls asked.

"Yeah. Hopefully! We'll be so cute up there, the two of us, right?" Caitlin watched as Brie leaned down. "Hey, what's that?"

"A daisy," one of the girls said. "A very sad, wilted daisy. Didn't you get one? That girl you sit next to in homeroom was passing them out this morning. I guess she's running for class president?"

"Oh yeah," Brie said. "She told me about that. Did you guys see her poster? It was so lame compared to the others. And get this, you guys. She wants to start a friendship club. Can you believe that?"

The other girls laughed. One of them said, "What is this, second grade?"

Tears pricked Caitlin's eyes, but she blinked them back. And here she'd thought that Brie had liked her idea of a friendship club.

How could she have been so stupid to think it was a good idea?

"Shhh," Brie said. "Quiet. Look, Lavinia's going up. Cross your fingers for her."

The teacher, Mrs. Sears, handed Lavinia a piece of paper and asked her to read some lines from the play's script. Caitlin thought Lavinia did an amazing job. She put a lot of emotion into the part, and it didn't sound like she was reading at all.

When she was finished, the teacher asked Lavinia what song she'd like to sing for the musical portion of the tryout.

A wave of panic hit Caitlin. She grabbed her backpack and pulled out the now crumpled piece of paper she'd gotten about her audition time. When she'd received the envelope in homeroom, she'd opened it and quickly glanced at it, noting the time, and then threw it in her backpack to look at later. Except, she'd forgotten to look at it later. The campaign had kept her busier than she'd thought it would.

Now, she read over the note and saw that Mrs. Sears had given a choice of five songs to choose from and indicated where they could find online music and samples of the songs being sung.

She didn't know any of the songs. Of course, she'd heard of them, but she wouldn't be able to get up there and sing them. The angry bees stung Caitlin's stomach as she tried to figure out what she was going to say when the teacher asked her what song she'd like to sing.

"Old MacDonald Had a Farm"?

"London Bridge Is Falling Down"?

"You Are My Sunshine"?

They were songs Caitlin knew by heart and could sing easily, but talk about second grade.

Mrs. Sears sat down at the piano and began to play. When Lavinia started singing her song, she sounded polished and professional. Like she'd been practicing for months, not days. Like she was born to play the part of Charlotte. Like no matter what Caitlin did, there was no way she could compete.

Caitlin started to get up to leave, but she didn't have a tight grip on her backpack and dropped it, causing Brie and her two friends to turn around.

"Sorry," Caitlin whispered.

"You're trying out?" Brie whispered.

Caitlin knew she had to say yes. Otherwise, they'd ask her what she was doing there, and what would she say? Auditions weren't open for just anyone to watch. It was hard enough without a bunch of random people in the audience.

Caitlin simply nodded and sat back down. There was no

way out. She had to go through with it. She could only hope that the girls would be finished first and leave, so they wouldn't see her terrible performance.

When Lavinia finished singing, her three friends whistled and yelled and gave her a standing ovation. Lavinia took a little bow and then hopped down off the stage and ran to her friends, who greeted her with hugs and high fives.

"Next we have Caitlin," Mrs. Sears called out. "Caitlin, are you here?"

Oh no. Already?

Caitlin knew there was nothing to do now but go up and get it over with.

"Yeah," she called out. "I'm here."

As Caitlin walked toward the stage, she ran her fingers along the charm bracelet and wished for it to finally bring her some good luck. She needed it now more than ever.

Onstage, Mrs. Sears handed her the page to read, just like she'd done with Lavinia. Caitlin did her best to read the lines loudly, with confidence and with emotion. When it was over, she felt pretty good about it. But of course, that had been the easy part.

"What song would you like to sing?" Mrs. Sears asked. "You read over the list of choices, right?"

"Um, I'm really sorry, but I lost the sheet you sent to me. While I was sitting there, waiting, I was trying to think of songs I know by heart, that you would know too. The only one I can think of is 'Frosty the Snowman.' Could we maybe do that one?"

Snickers erupted throughout the auditorium.

"Quiet, ladies and gentlemen," Mrs. Sears said. "There will be none of that during auditions or I'll make you all wait for your turn in the hallway." She turned and smiled at Caitlin. "That will be fine. I like that song."

Mrs. Sears sat down at the piano and began to play. And as Caitlin sang about a snowman, in September, with his corncob pipe and his button nose, she wondered if maybe she could just move to the North Pole and go to the school there.

Chapter 16

Zinnia
a favorite of songbirds

"Do you have any money?" Caitlin asked her brother. This time she found him on his bed, reading a graphic novel.

"Are you trying to be funny?" Isaac asked. "If you are, that's not funny at all."

Caitlin sat down on Isaac's bed. "I assume that's a no?"

"I don't have any money to give you, but do you need any more jokes?" he asked.

Caitlin shrugged. "I could use a good laugh right about now. Sure. Give it to me."

"Where do snowmen keep their money?" Isaac asked.

"Oh no," Caitlin said. "Not a snowman joke. Anything but a snowman joke."

Isaac continued on, oblivious. "A snowbank." He slapped

her on the knee. "Isn't that funny? Come on, laugh, would ya?"

Caitlin smiled. Barely. "Sorry. I can't. Today was the worst day ever."

"People didn't like your posters?" he asked.

"I don't even think they noticed my posters," Caitlin said.

Just then, Jessi poked her head into Isaac's room. "Can I come in?"

"Oh good," Caitlin said. "You're home. Do *you* have any money?"

Jessi came in and shut the door. "Yeah. Sure. Drawers full. Gold or silver coins, take your pick."

"Coins?" Isaac asked.

"Yeah," Jessi said, crossing her arms. "You know, from the buried treasure I found yesterday with the band of pirates."

"Cool!" Isaac said. "Can I go next time?"

"Only if you don't get seasick," Jessi said. She looked at her sister. "What do you need money for?"

"I was hoping I could buy some fun-size candy bars and pass them out tomorrow at school," Caitlin explained. "For my class president campaign."

"Well, you can pretty much kiss that idea good-bye," Jessi said. She came over to the bed and motioned for Caitlin to scoot over, so she did. "Mom and Dad are downstairs talking. I heard Dad say that he heard through the grapevine at work that layoff notices are going out soon. Since he's a manager, and no one is talking to him about it, he's pretty sure he'll be getting one."

Isaac jumped off the bed, ran to his closet, went inside, and shut the door.

Jessi gave her sister a curious look. "What's he doing?"

"Hiding from zombies," Caitlin said. Then she whispered, "That's where he goes when he's scared. You shouldn't have told him that. About Dad's job."

"I thought you guys would want to know. I mean, the coming days are gonna be tense. I plan to be around as little as possible." Jessi stood up. "If I were you, I would tread carefully around them. And definitely don't ask for money unless you need it for something really important."

"Are you trying to tell me winning the class president spot isn't important?"

"No," she said. "But trying to win it by buying kids candy isn't." She went to the door. "If I had some extra money, I'd loan it to you. But I don't. Just write a really

126

good speech. One that wows them. That's what matters the most anyway. Trust me." Before she left she said, "Good luck."

Caitlin sighed. "Yeah. Thanks."

She went to the closet and opened the door. "Isaac? Come out and go back to reading your book. Don't hide in there. Everything's going to be okay."

"No it's not," he said. "The zombies are coming. Soon they'll break down the door and smash the windows, and that's it. We're goners."

"There's no such thing as zombies, Isaac."

"You can believe what you want, Caitlin. But I believe in them. And I'm staying in here, where it's safe." He paused. "Or until I get hungry, anyway."

The next morning, Caitlin went to her locker and found Esther there, getting her books.

"Did you get the candy bars?" Esther asked her. "I'll help you pass them out, if you want me to."

"No. I couldn't scrounge up any money. And my mom says she already spent enough money on my campaign."

"Oh. Sorry. Well, just work really hard on your speech.

It's probably the most important part of your campaign anyway."

"That's what my sister said. But I'm not sure. I mean, it feels like it's mostly just a popularity contest. And in case you haven't noticed, there's no way I'm going to win if that's what it really is."

"I saw you coming out of the auditorium yesterday," Esther said. "How'd your audition go?"

Caitlin moaned as she slammed the locker door. "Sorry, but I really don't want to talk about it. I'm kind of trying to forget it ever happened."

"I tried out too," Esther said as they started making their way to homeroom. "Since it's my first play, I'm hoping for one of the smaller parts. I just thought it'd be fun, since it's one of my favorite books."

"So, did you have to sing?" Caitlin asked

Esther shook her head. "No. Are you kidding me? Me and singing get along about as well as dogs and poetry."

Caitlin smiled. "Wait. Dogs can't recite poetry? But I love poetry. That would be so cool."

"Right?" Esther said. They reached the door of Mr. Hankins's classroom just as the first bell rang. "So are you working on your speech during class today?"

"If I have any chance at winning class president," Caitlin replied, "I think I'll be working on my speech every second I'm awake until the assembly on Thursday."

Esther gave Caitlin's arm a gentle squeeze. "I can't wait to hear it. I know it's going to be amazing."

If only I could be half as sure as that, Caitlin thought.

Chapter 17

Orchid
ONE iS all you Need

When they arrived at the soup kitchen Wednesday night, Caitlin could tell right away something wasn't quite right.

The first sign was that Mrs. Watson wasn't wearing her FRIENDLY EAR, RIGHT HERE button on her apron. In fact, her apron looked like she'd just thrown it on, as it was kind of wrinkly and hung a little crooked from her neck.

The second sign was that the kitchen was quiet. Like, test-taking quiet. No one talked like they usually did while they prepped the food.

Mrs. Watson greeted Mrs. Rogers, Caitlin, Jessi (her mom had insisted she come this time), and Isaac by simply saying, "Hello. Nice to see you. We're having spaghetti with bread and butter and salad tonight, so you'll get to help with the bread and salad again."

"That's just fine," Mrs. Rogers said. Then she leaned in and asked, "Is everything all right? Seems a bit somber here."

"Oh. Right. I'm sorry. I suppose I should tell all of you too. I got word today that our friend Sonny is in the hospital."

Both Isaac's and Caitlin's hands flew to their mouths as they let out little gasps. "Is he going to be okay?" Caitlin asked.

"I'm afraid I don't know much right now," Mrs. Watson said. "A nurse called me, at Sonny's request. He doesn't have any family nearby, so I gave him my number a long time ago and told him to call me if he ever needed anything. She said he wanted me to know he was in the hospital with a bad case of the flu and not to worry when I didn't see him come for dinner."

"What about Wilbur?" Isaac asked. "Who's taking care of him?"

Mrs. Watson patted Isaac's shoulder. "Don't worry. I went over to his place and checked. He has a neighbor in his apartment complex who's keeping an eye out on Wilbur."

Mrs. Rogers looked at her kids and said, "I know you care about Sonny and Wilbur, but try not to worry. He's in the hospital, where he'll get good care, and he's talking, obviously, if he told a nurse to call. Now we should get the food ready for everyone else who needs it tonight, right?"

And with that, Mrs. Watson showed them to their spots so they could get to work. When it was time for Caitlin and Isaac to pass out cookies and bread, Isaac said, "Remember how Sonny asked for two cookies, just so we could have one when we were finished?"

"I remember," Caitlin said. "I know you're upset, but try to put it out of your mind, okay? We can't have cookies with tears. That would be so . . ."

"Soggy?" Isaac said.

It made Caitlin laugh. "Well, I was going to say sad, but yeah, soggy too."

A few minutes later, Tezra came through the line, looking a little bit like a soggy cookie herself. "Did you hear the news?" Tezra asked Caitlin.

Caitlin nodded. "Yeah. Do you know him very well?"

Tezra nodded. "We've sat with him quite a few times. He's so nice. Just last week he was talking about wanting to come and see *Charlotte's Web* at our school."

"Yeah," Caitlin said. "He told me that too. Did you try out for the play?"

"Come on, honey," her mom said. "Let's go sit down."

"Can you come over and talk to me when you're done?" Tezra asked. "We'll wait for you. I never see you at school. I've looked for you a couple of times. Where do you sit at lunch?"

"The reading table," Caitlin said, feeling funny as she said it.

"Oh. I didn't look there. Well, come find me when you're finished, 'kay?"

"Okay."

"I told you so," Isaac said. "Remember? Last time? I told you she wants to be your friend."

"I don't know. I think she just wants to talk about Sonny. She's upset, like you."

"Well," Isaac said, "she could talk to her mom if she wanted to talk to just anybody. But she wants to talk to *you*. Plus, she was looking for you at school."

When all of the people had been served, Caitlin asked her mom if she could go sit with Tezra for a few minutes. "She asked me to," Caitlin explained. "I don't want to be rude."

"All right. For a few minutes. Then come back here and help us clean up."

"I will."

When Caitlin walked over, Tezra jumped up out of her seat and said, "Mom, I'll be back in a few minutes, 'kay? We're gonna be over here." She pointed at an empty table.

Her mom gave her a little nod before she went back to talking to the lady sitting next to her.

The girls sat down across from each other.

"Isn't it sad?" Tezra said, her pretty eyes full of concern. "I hope he's okay."

"I know," Caitlin said. "Me too."

"Everyone's talking about him," Tezra said. "It's amazing how this place has become like family to so many of us."

"That's pretty cool," Caitlin said.

"You know, I hate to say this, but I don't even know your name," she said.

"Oh, right. Sorry, it's Caitlin. Caitlin Rogers."

Tezra sat back and crossed her arms. "Wait. I know that name. I saw it on one of the posters. It had balloons on it. You're running for class president?"

Caitlin felt her cheeks get warm. "Yeah. Except at this point, I know there's practically zero chance that I'll win."

"Why do you say that?"

Caitlin ticked the reasons off on her fingers. "Basically, I'm not funny enough, popular enough, or rich enough."

Tezra moaned. "It *is* pretty much a popularity contest, isn't it? I hate that. Well, let me know if there's anything I can do to help you, 'kay? Is your speech ready for the assembly tomorrow?"

"I still need to work on it when I get home."

"I'm sure it's going to be amazing," Tezra said. "I can't wait to hear it. And you know I'll vote for you."

"Thanks." Caitlin looked at the clock on the wall and stood up. "I better go help clean up so we can leave pretty soon."

Tezra stood up too. "I'm so glad we got to talk for a few minutes. Oh, and you asked if I tried out for the school play. I did, but not for a singing part. I'd love to be in it, I just don't sing very well. Did you try out?"

Caitlin grimaced. "Yeah, but I don't think I have a chance at the part I really want. Maybe I can be Sonny's date to the play and sit and watch you and everyone else. It sounds like it's going to be super-cute." She waved. "See ya later."

"See ya."

When Caitlin reached her family, her mom turned and smiled at her. "She seems like a nice girl, huh?"

"Yeah," Caitlin said. "She's really nice. And she said she'll vote for me tomorrow."

Jessi turned to her and said, "So one down, and hundreds to go?"

"Yep," Caitlin said as she grabbed a towel so she could help dry the dishes they were washing. "Pretty much."

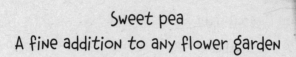

Chapter 18

Sweet pea
A fine addition to any flower garden

After Caitlin and her family had soup and sandwiches for dinner, she went straight to her room. She lay on her bed, thinking about everything that happened in the past week.

The daisy disaster.

The awful audition.

Pink-slip possibilities.

And Sonny's horrible hospital news.

It was a week full of bad news. And alliteration apparently. The more she thought about all the things that had gone wrong, the angrier she became. She reached underneath the long-sleeve shirt she wore, unclasped the charm bracelet, and threw it on the floor.

Her phone buzzed, so she picked it up. Jade wanted to video chat. Maybe it would cheer her up, she thought. It certainly wouldn't make her feel any worse. She accepted the call.

"I figured you probably needed a motivational speech right about now," Jade said.

"You figured right," Caitlin said.

"Do you want the long version or the short version?"

"Short, please. I still have a lot of work to do."

"Okay. Here it goes." Jade pointed her finger at Caitlin. "You can do this. You have what it takes to lead the sixth grade to greatness. This is about more than how funny your poster is, Caitlin. This is about how you have the ability to change that school for the better."

Caitlin pressed her lips together. She didn't know if she should laugh or cry at how hard her friend was trying to help her.

"But what if I'm not cut out for greatness?" Caitlin said. "I mean, maybe I should just transfer out when the quarter's over. Go to your school."

"But you like your classes, don't you?" Jade asked.

"Yeah. I love my drama class. And my English class. Okay, pretty much all of them, since I transferred out of the horrifying dance class. But the rest of it . . . I don't know. Nothing's turning out the way I thought it would."

"Hey, remember that time a few years ago when we wanted to make chocolate chip cookies, but we didn't have any chocolate chips? So your mom said we should try making snickerdoodles instead. And we were like, what are snickerdoodles, and she couldn't believe we'd never had snickerdoodles. So we made them, and they turned out awesome. Remember that?"

"Yeah," Caitlin replied.

"Sometimes awesome shows up when you least expect it."

"Did you read that on a refrigerator magnet?" Caitlin asked.

Jade smiled as if she'd just been handed a plate of snickerdoodles. "No, I made it up. Right now. For you."

"Maybe I'll put that in my speech."

"You totally should."

"I gotta go," Caitlin said with a sigh.

"I know. Can you stop by after school tomorrow?"

"No. I have a Battle of the Books meeting. But I'll be sure and let you know how the speech goes."

"Sounds good."

"Okay. Bye."

"Good luck! You can do it!"

Caitlin turned off her phone so she wouldn't be distracted anymore. Then someone knocked on her door. So much for no distractions.

"Come in!"

Her mom came in with an envelope in her hand. "I just picked up the mail. This came for you today."

Caitlin jumped up and grabbed the envelope from her mom's hand. She read the return address and smiled when she saw it was from Mia. "Thanks, Mom."

"Hey, what's this?" her mom asked as she walked over and picked up the bracelet off the floor.

"It's, um, a charm bracelet," Caitlin said, kicking herself for being so careless. "My camp friends and I bought it together on a field trip. We're supposed to pass it around and add charms to it. I didn't tell you about it because I wasn't sure if you would be mad that I spent the money you gave me, when you're trying so hard to save money."

"I'm not mad," her mom said. "It was your money to spend at camp. In fact, I think it's real sweet, sharing it with your three friends. But why's it on the floor?"

"I kind of got upset," Caitlin said, softly. "About all the bad stuff that's been happening. I guess I took it out on the bracelet."

Mrs. Rogers handed the bracelet to Caitlin. "My mother used to tell me, it's always darkest before the dawn." She gave Caitlin a big, long hug. "Hang in there, honey. This is when it's important to count your blessings. We're fortunate to have a roof over our heads and food on the table. And you have lots of people who care about you. Remember that, okay?" Caitlin nodded. "Do your best tomorrow. That's all you can do. When all is said and done, if you've done that, you can hold your head high, no matter what happens."

"Thanks, Mom."

"Your dad and I, we really are proud of you. How you're trying so hard to get involved in things at school."

"Did I hear my name?" Caitlin's dad poked his head in. "She's right. We are proud of you, Peaches. You'll do a marvelous job tomorrow, I'm sure of it. I wish I could come and watch."

"No!" Caitlin said. "Having my parents there would be even worse than having lame posters. I'll be fine."

"You'll be better than fine," her dad said. "Just let the real you come shining through."

After her mom and dad left, Caitlin opened up the envelope. She pulled out a picture Mia had taken of the four girls with her camera, using the timer. They were standing on the porch of the cabin, their arms around each other. It made Caitlin tear up, because it kind of hurt, how much she missed them.

After she stared at the photo for a long time, she read Mia's letter.

DEAR CAITLIN,
HEY! HOW ARE YOU?
SORRY IT'S TAKEN ME A WHILE TO WRITE TO YOU. I KIND OF HAD AN ACCIDENT AFTER I GOT HOME. I MEAN, NOTHING HORRIBLE, LIKE BEING ATTACKED BY A SHARK OR HAVING MY BRAINS SMASHED IN DURING A SURFING ACCIDENT. ALTHOUGH I KIND OF WISH IT WAS SOMETHING EXCITING LIKE THAT, BECAUSE IT'S SO EMBARRASSING TO SAY WHAT ACTUALLY HAPPENED. IT SOUNDS LIKE I'M THE CLUMSIEST PERSON IN THE WORLD, AND MAYBE I AM, BUT NOW SO MANY MORE PEOPLE ACTUALLY KNOW THAT I'M CLUMSY.

I WAS HELPING MY MOM GET SOMETHING IN A CUPBOARD UP HIGH IN THE CAFÉ (BECAUSE I HELP HER THERE SOMETIMES, YOU KNOW), AND I FELL OFF THE STEP STOOL. YES. YOU READ THAT RIGHT. CAN YOU BELIEVE IT? I

MISSED THE BOTTOM STEP, LANDED FUNNY, AND BROKE A BONE IN MY FOOT. NOW I'M IN A WALKING CAST, SO AT LEAST IT'S NOT TOO HARD TO GET AROUND, BUT IT'S STILL TERRIBLE BECAUSE I AM OFFICIALLY OUT FOR THE REST OF THE SOCCER SEASON. NOT TO MENTION I CAN'T SURF <u>AT ALL</u> WITH THIS STUPID THING ON MY LEG.

SINCE ALL OF MY FRIENDS ARE BUSY DOING THINGS I CAN'T DO, I'VE BEEN SPENDING A LOT OF TIME READING MY CAMP JOURNAL TO CHEER MYSELF UP. DO YOU REMEMBER THIS QUESTION OF THE DAY:

WHAT DO YOU THINK IS THE MOST IMPORTANT QUALITY IN A FRIEND?

YOU ANSWERED THAT QUESTION IN MY JOURNAL, AND I LOVE WHAT YOU WROTE. YOU SAID, "SOMEONE WHO ACCEPTS YOU JUST THE WAY YOU ARE. IT CAN BE EASY TO GET CAUGHT UP ON THINGS THAT DON'T REALLY MATTER THAT MUCH. BUT THE ABILITY TO BE YOURSELF, DURING GOOD TIMES AND BAD, IS SO IMPORTANT. AND A GOOD FRIEND WON'T JUDGE YOU. SHE'LL JUST CARE ABOUT YOU, NO MATTER WHAT."

THANK YOU FOR LETTING ME BE MYSELF, AND FOR BEING MY FRIEND. I GOT THE LETTER YOU WROTE ME, AND I HOPE BY NOW YOU'VE MADE SOME NEW FRIENDS AT YOUR

SCHOOL — GIRLS WHO CAN ACCEPT YOU JUST THE WAY YOU ARE.

Do you LIKE THE PICTURE I'M SENDING ALONG? I LOVE IT. I'M SENDING IT TO LIBBY AND HANNAH TOO. I BOUGHT A LITTLE FRAME FOR MINE, AND IT SITS NEXT TO MY BED. I LOOK AT IT EVERY DAY AND REMEMBER ALL THE GOOD TIMES WE HAD TOGETHER. THE FOUR OF US SURE DID A GREAT JOB OF ACCEPTING EACH OTHER FOR WHO WE ARE, RIGHT?

I HOPE THE BRACELET IS BRINGING YOU LOTS OF LUCK. WRITE BACK SOON!

YOUR CABIN 7 BFF,
MIA

Caitlin opened her fist and looked at the bracelet she'd held since her mother had handed it to her. What had Hannah said, that day in the Pink Giraffe? *It feels nice and strong. Just like our friendship.*

Something told her to put it back on. To not give up on it yet. To not give up, period. As she put the bracelet back on her wrist, she saw the four girls sitting around the friendship circle, reading poetry from the book Caitlin had brought along. They hadn't laughed at her when she'd shared it with them. They hadn't said that poetry was weird or boring or any of the other things they could have said. They'd asked her why she liked it. What was it about this book that was special to her? And they'd listened when she told them she loved how each poem featured a flower, because she was crazy for flowers. Each page was beautifully illustrated, and she'd always felt like it was more than a book — it was almost like having a little flower garden all her own.

She looked over at the rose that was still in the vase by her bed. It was starting to wither up and die. That was the problem with cut flowers. They didn't last long. Her eyes wandered up to the poster of the flower growing through the sidewalk.

And that's when it hit her — the perfect ending to her speech.

Chapter 19

PANSY
when it blooms, it smiles

The assembly was first thing in the morning, during homeroom. As they walked to the auditorium, Esther walked alongside Caitlin, while the four fun girls walked ahead, whispering back and forth among themselves. Earlier, Caitlin had seen they all wore buttons that said YOUR VOTE FOR DELLA IS PRICELESS.

Suddenly, Caitlin wanted to run the other way. Go to the office and tell the nurse she was having a migraine and needed to lie down in the dark with a cold rag on her forehead. Yes, she'd finished her speech, but what was the point? There was no way she would win. And there was no way the fun girls would ever let her into their group.

"It's hopeless," she muttered.

"No," Esther said. "It's not." She reached out with a closed fist. "Here. This is for you. To bring you luck."

Caitlin held out her hand, and Esther dropped a tiny pink paper star into her palm.

"Did you make this?" Caitlin asked her.

"Yes. It's an origami lucky star. I love making them. I can show you how sometime, if you'd like. You can make them in different colors and then put them in a glass jar or vase. Cute, right?"

Caitlin examined the star closely. It was light as air, and puffy. She couldn't see any tape or glue, just places where the paper had been folded.

"That's amazing," Caitlin told her as she slipped the star into the pocket of her skirt. "Thank you so much."

"You're welcome."

As the kids streamed into the auditorium, Caitlin saw Tezra waving at her from across the sea of people. She waved back and realized that talking to Esther and seeing Tezra made her feel better.

She thought about the letter from Mia yesterday. How she'd answered that question of the day in the journal all those weeks ago.

Friends let you be yourself and they care about you, no matter what.

Caitlin breathed a sigh of relief. No matter what happened today, it didn't really matter anymore. She *did* have friends. Every day she'd talked to Esther at their locker. Esther had listened to Caitlin go on and on about her campaign and speech, and listened like nothing else was as important as Caitlin. It was as if she'd been wearing Mrs. Watson's button. And what had Caitlin done in return, for Esther? Not a thing. She'd been too focused on getting in with the fun girls to realize she had a wonderful friend right in front of her.

She had to make it up to her. Somehow, some way, she would make it up to her. Starting today.

The students took their seats and Caitlin silently read over her speech one more time, while others talked around her. She took a pencil and scribbled in a new line. A few minutes later, the principal, Mr. Eckhart, took the stage and rambled on about the importance of learning about politics through the student body election process. Caitlin didn't listen very closely. She was telling herself things like:

Stay calm.

Talk slowly.

Make sure to breathe.

When he finished his talk, he told the audience the order for the speeches would be sixth graders, then seventh graders, and finally eighth graders.

"Only vice presidential and presidential candidates will give speeches, due to time constraints, though later today you will be voting on treasurer and secretary for your grades as well. Each of the candidates will speak for approximately three minutes. This should be ample time for them to give you an idea of the kind of leadership they would offer the school. I expect everyone to be kind and courteous to every single candidate during the speeches. All right, sixth-grade vice presidential candidates, please take the stage!"

The vice presidential candidates for sixth grade went up and sat down in the three chairs in the middle of the stage. Mr. Eckhart said they would go in alphabetical order, so that meant Marcus Bailey would go first.

Marcus approached the podium and started talking into the microphone. His voice was soft. So soft, that even with the microphone, Caitlin could hardly hear him.

"You'll have to speak up, Marcus," Mr. Eckhart told him.

He spoke louder, but his voice shook. Caitlin fidgeted in her seat, feeling sorry for him. Why did they have to do speeches anyway? She was pretty sure most kids would rather do a weekend's worth of homework than have to endure giving a speech to the entire student body.

The next candidate wasn't as nervous. She even made the kids laugh a couple of times. The final candidate said about twenty words and then sat back down. Short, sweet, and to the point. Caitlin wondered for a second if maybe she should try that tactic. *No*, she told herself. *Stick to the plan.*

"All right, thank you," Mr. Eckhart said. "Next we'll have the presidential candidates for sixth grade take the stage, please."

Esther smiled at Caitlin as she stood up. Caitlin told herself to look over this way while she talked, at Esther's kind and encouraging eyes.

The three candidates took their seats onstage. Caitlin figured out that based on their last names, Kristopher would go first, then Caitlin, and finally Della. When the principal said Kristopher's name, a section in the auditorium way in the back went crazy, yelling and clapping. They were all boys. Loud boys.

Kristopher's whole speech was filled with *Star Wars* quotes. He got lots of laughs and applause. Caitlin thought it was kind of ridiculous. When he was finished, the section of boys yelled even louder.

Caitlin resisted the urge to roll her eyes.

"Thank you, Kristopher," Mr. Eckhart. "Our next presidential candidate is Caitlin Rogers."

Caitlin felt like a rubber chicken, weird and wobbly, as she made her way across the stage. A few people were clapping, but not many. Caitlin placed her paper on the podium before she looked out at the sea of faces. She swallowed hard.

"When I started school here, more than anything else, I wanted to make friends. None of my friends from elementary school are here, so making friends was my number one priority. People told me the best way to make friends was to get involved in activities, and at first, that's why I decided to run for class president. I thought if I got elected president, I'd be the cool girl. The girl everyone wants to be friends with.

"But as time went by, I realized that really wasn't a good reason to become class president. And just today, I realized I've already made some friends. I've been so wrapped up in this campaign and winning and getting in with a group of girls who looked like fun, I didn't see what was right in front of me. So thank you, Esther, for everything you've done for me. And Tezra, after we talked earlier in the week, I feel like we're on our way to becoming friends too, and I'm so happy about that. Another friend told me last night, sometimes awesome shows up when you least expect it, and I know she's right.

"So now that I have some friends, what am I hoping for? I'm hoping to make this school the best it can be. A place where kids feel safe and happy and accepted, no matter who they are, what they look like, or how much money their parents make. If I'm elected your class president, I will talk to the administration about how important it is to make this school a place where we don't knock others down but pick each other up. A place where kindness is treated like a flower garden — the more we work on making it grow, the better it will be.

"I have a poster in my room that says, 'Bloom where you are planted.' We're all planted here, at this great school where we are encouraged to do activities we love, like art or dance or music or theater. I hope we can all grow and bloom together. Thank you."

Everyone clapped as Caitlin turned around and walked back toward her seat. Maybe no one yelled for her like they'd yelled for Kristopher, but Caitlin felt good. She'd done it. And she'd done it without passing out or throwing up or dying from stage fright.

After the speeches were over, the students were excused and told to make way to their second-period classes. Both Tezra and Esther waited outside the auditorium doors for Caitlin, showering her with compliments when she appeared.

"It was *so* good," Tezra said.

"Amazing," Esther said. "And I can't believe you mentioned me."

"Me neither," Tezra said. "It was really sweet of you."

Caitlin realized the two girls might not know each other, so she quickly introduced them.

"Do you like to read?" Esther asked Tezra.

"Yes, I do."

"Do you want to be on our Battle of the Books team?" Esther asked. "Someone dropped out yesterday, so I've been looking for a new member. We're meeting today after school."

Tezra smiled. "I'd love that. Thanks for asking me."

As the three girls walked down the hall together, Caitlin took her speech notes and threw them in a recycling bin. She was so glad it was over.

But more than that, she was glad she didn't have to worry about trying to get involved in any more activities, unless she really wanted to. Because for now, she had all the friends she needed.

Chapter 20

Lilac
the pretty scent is such a sweet surprise

$\mathcal{E}$sther's mom gave Caitlin a ride home after the Battle of the Books meeting. When they pulled into the driveway, Caitlin's heart dropped to her stomach. Her dad was home early again.

After she said good-bye to Esther and her mom, Caitlin got out and slowly walked to the door. She waved to Esther as they pulled away. Then she stopped walking, hoping to calm down before she went inside. Last time, when her dad had come home early, she'd been wrong about the reason. But what could it be now? Her dad didn't need to go to the dentist again for at least six months.

She had a feeling that this time, it really meant something.

Hoping to hear her family before they heard her, she opened the door slowly. And then she gasped.

"Surprise!" her family shouted, the family room decorated with balloons and streamers.

Caitlin stood there, taking it all in, trying to decide what it meant.

"But . . . it's not my birthday," she said.

Her dad laughed. "Of course it isn't, Peaches. We're celebrating your successful speech today."

She narrowed her eyes. "How do you know it was successful?"

"Because your homeroom teacher, Mr. Hankins, sent us an e-mail," Mrs. Rogers said. "He wanted us to know what an incredible job you did and that he was so impressed with what you had to say."

"You must have mentioned me, your incredible brother, in your speech, right, Caitlin?" Isaac teased.

Caitlin put her backpack on the floor near the door. "I can't believe you guys did this for me."

"We have a cake too," Isaac said. He looked over at Jessi. "What kind is it again?"

"Pineapple upside-down cake," she replied. She stood off to the side, her arms crossed, like she was annoyed to be wasting time standing there. "With real whipped cream. Can I go back upstairs, Mom?"

"No," Mr. Rogers said. "While you're all here, there's something I want to tell you."

Caitlin gulped. This was it. The moment they'd been waiting for. Dreading. Of course he'd tell them all he came home early to celebrate. That way he could break the news to them gently.

She looked over at Isaac, expecting him to take off for his closet any second. He didn't seem to be concerned. Still, once her dad told them, she knew that's what he'd do. While Isaac stared at their dad, waiting to hear what it was he wanted to tell them, Caitlin walked over to her little brother and put her arm around his shoulders.

"I know it hasn't been easy, being on a tight budget and wondering what might happen with my job. You've been worried, I know, and I'm sorry. I've been interviewing almost every week, but nothing's panned out."

The suspense was killing Caitlin. She couldn't stand it. "Just tell us," she said. "Please, Dad. Just tell us you lost your job today and get it over with."

He shook his head. "No, that's not what I want to tell you. Not at all. In fact, it's just the opposite. You see, I don't have to interview anymore, and you don't have to worry anymore, because my job is safe. Layoff packets were handed out today, and I didn't get one. My boss pulled me into his office today and told me I have nothing to worry about."

"Woo-hoo!" Isaac yelled, running over to his dad and jumping into his arms. "Does this mean we can get the good TV channels again?"

Their dad laughed. "I think it does, little buddy."

Both Jessi and Caitlin stood there, like they could hardly believe the news.

"Isn't it wonderful?" Mrs. Rogers said. "We can go shopping this weekend, and get you all some new clothes."

Caitlin clapped her hands together at the thought. Isaac, on the other hand, who didn't like shopping for clothes, groaned.

"Isaac, come help me with dinner," Mrs. Rogers said, turning toward the kitchen. "It's your turn. Girls, it'll be ready in about thirty minutes."

Mr. Rogers walked over and gave Caitlin a big hug. "It's a good day, isn't it, baby girl?" He looked over at Jessi. "Come over here. Group hug. What do you say?"

Caitlin expected Jessi to nix that idea, but she actually

came over and put her arms around both of them. "I love you girls," he told them. "Thanks for hanging in there."

"You know, Dad," Jessi said. "There's this new phone a lot of my friends have. Do you think —"

He started laughing. "Just because I still have my job doesn't mean I'm Mr. Moneybags all of a sudden. Your current phone does the job just fine."

Jessi shrugged and then turned to go upstairs. "You can't blame me for trying, right?"

"We'll never know unless we try," Mr. Rogers said. "That's exactly right." He looked down at Caitlin. "And now we'll see if you get enough votes to be sixth-grade class president."

"I don't think I'll win," Caitlin said. "But it's okay. Everything worked out."

"What about that play?" her dad asked. "When are the roles announced for that?"

"We find out about both the election and the play on Monday," Caitlin said.

Her dad smiled. "Good thing you'll be doing a bunch of shopping. I suspect it'll be one terribly long weekend, waiting to get all that news."

"I don't think I'll win the election or get a part," Caitlin said. "But I can't lie. I'm really curious how it's all going to turn out."

Mr. Rogers held up his two hands with his fingers crossed. "All we can do is try our hardest — then hope for the best."

Chapter 21

Snapdragon
Not as fierce as you might think

On Saturday, Caitlin, her mom, and her two siblings hopped in the minivan to head to the mall. Jessi sat in the front passenger seat, while Caitlin and Isaac sat together in the middle seat.

Isaac tapped Caitlin on the knee. She turned to him. "I took my fort down. You know, the one in my closet?"

Caitlin smiled. "Are the zombies gone?"

"I think so," he said. "I hope so."

"Me too," Caitlin said.

"Do you ever get scared of things?" he asked her as he ran his finger over the Hot Wheels car he'd brought along.

"Yeah."

"What do you do when you're scared of something?" Isaac asked.

Caitlin looked out the window and thought about that for a minute. Then she turned to him and said, "I talk about it with friends. Or, you know, someone who cares about me."

"Don't they laugh at you? Call you a fraidycat or something?"

"Little brother, if they laugh at you, they're not really your friends, right?" She leaned in and whispered, "And you know, you can always talk to me. I promise, I'll never laugh at you."

"Okay. Well, here's something I want to talk about. I'm afraid Mom is going to forget to call and get the good channels turned back on."

Caitlin smiled. "Did you hear that, Mom?" she asked.

Mrs. Rogers stopped at a stoplight, then turned around. "There's nothing to be afraid of, sweetie. I called yesterday. Should be good to go by Monday."

Isaac did a fist pump in the air. "Yes!"

As Isaac turned back to playing with his car, Caitlin thought about how lucky she was to have friends she could talk to.

Jade, who'd helped her so much with her campaign and had stayed so positive about it all.

Esther and Tezra, who'd both been really encouraging, at just the right times.

And, of course, Mia, Hannah, and Libby. Each of them had believed in her ability to make friends more than Caitlin had. And every time she'd thought of them, it had reminded her that although finding and making friends might not always be easy, in the end, it was so worth it.

Caitlin fingered the bracelet and knew today was the day she needed to get a charm. It was time to send it off to the next person. She'd already decided whom she'd send it to. Mia had a broken foot and Caitlin wanted so much to do something that would cheer her up. She'd send the bracelet along with a package of cookies or something. If only she could send a fruit pizza. The thought made Caitlin smile. Now that would cheer her up!

When they got to the mall, Jessi asked if she could just get some money and go off on her own.

"I figured that's what you'd want to do," Mrs. Rogers said as she reached into her purse. She pulled out two envelopes and handed one to each of the girls. "You two can go together and buy what you need while I take Isaac to try on some things. Let's meet by the big glass elevators in two hours. That will be twelve thirty. We'll grab some lunch in the food court, and then if there are more things you need to get, we'll go together. How's that?"

Caitlin nodded enthusiastically as she peeked inside the envelope before sticking it in her purse. It couldn't have worked out more perfectly. This way, she could get some clothes, hopefully on sale, and then shop for the charm with the money she had left over.

"All right," Mrs. Rogers said. "Please, be safe. Try and stick together. And call me if you need anything, all right?"

"We'll be fine, Mom," Jessi said. "We're at the mall, not the state penitentiary."

"Can we go to the LEGO store, Mom?" Isaac asked. "Please, please, please?"

"Because you don't have enough LEGOS in your room to pick up and put away?" Mrs. Rogers teased. "I suppose we can make a quick stop in there. But just to look. Your birthday's coming up in a couple of months, you know."

They turned and left, and then Caitlin asked Jessi, "So, where do you want to go?"

Her sister stuck the envelope into her little black purse. "Well, I'm going to that adorable store Just Between Friends. I don't know where you're going."

"Jessi, Mom said we should stick together."

"Whatever. I prefer to shop alone. But you can shop there too, if you want to. Or not. I mean, you're a big girl. You can decide what you want to do."

Jessi turned and started walking. Caitlin hung back but followed her. It probably wasn't cool to be seen with your little sister at the mall. Caitlin wondered why she couldn't have a sister who was also her friend. Her mother had told her once, when Jessi had been particularly mean to Caitlin for some silly little thing, that it wouldn't be this way forever. Just because they weren't really friends now didn't mean they never would be, she'd said.

The girls shopped in the store for more than an hour but kept their distance from each other. Caitlin mostly shopped the sale racks and wound up with two new pairs of jeans, a couple of skirts, and some new tops. She still had some money left to buy a charm, and that's what she wanted to shop for next. What she didn't know was whether she should tell Jessi about the charm bracelet.

While she waited for her sister to finish shopping, Caitlin stood out front, eyeing the big department store just a few stores down. That's where she wanted to go. She figured she'd have the most luck finding a charm there.

When her sister finally emerged, they only had twenty

more minutes until they needed to meet up with their mom and brother. Caitlin decided to tell Jessi the truth.

"Did you get some good stuff?" Caitlin asked, trying to be nice.

"Thankfully, yes."

"I was wondering if we could go look at some jewelry next. I need to get a charm for my bracelet." Caitlin held out her arm so Jessi could see what she was talking about.

"Oh, that's pretty," she said. "When'd you get that?"

"At camp. Four of us girls went in on it together, and we're kind of sharing it. I'm supposed to buy a charm and then send it on to another girl to wear."

Caitlin waited for Jessi to laugh at her, or to make some smart remark about how childish it was to share a bracelet.

But she didn't do either.

"Wow," she said. "I love that. It's like a way to keep your camp friends close until you see each other again." She paused. "You know, I'm sort of jealous of your ability to make friends so easily. I mean, look at how you already fit in at your new school. For the past few weeks, I've been having trouble getting along with my friends, who I've known forever."

Maybe that was why Jessi had been acting so grouchy. "I'm sorry," Caitlin said. "Is there anything I can do?"

"I don't think so," she said with a sigh. "I'm gonna see if Mom will let me have them over for pizza and a movie tomorrow afternoon. Pizza will make things better, don't you think?"

Caitlin thought of her four friends at camp and that fruit pizza they'd loved so much. "Definitely," she said. Then she had an idea. "How about if I make a super-delicious dessert for you and your friends? Something amazing that will make them forget why they were ever upset with you."

"You'd do that for me?" she asked.

"Jessi, friends are important," Caitlin said. "I want to help you. Besides, I hate seeing you so miserable all the time."

"What are you going to make?"

Caitlin didn't want to tell her. She wanted the fruit pizza to be a surprise. "Something I had at camp. It's really good. You'll see."

"So," Jessi said, "what kind of charm are you going to get, do you know?"

"A flower," Caitlin responded as they started walking toward the department store together.

Jessi nodded. "Let me guess. Because you've had to figure out how to bloom where you're planted?"

It made Caitlin smile. Her sister knew her well. Better than either of them would probably ever admit. "Exactly."

Maybe, Caitlin thought, there was hope for the two of them to be friends someday after all.

Chapter 22

Poppy
worn with pride

$\mathcal{M}$onday morning, Caitlin told herself she shouldn't be nervous. There was no way she was going to win the election.

And yet, as she got ready for school, she was a bundle of nerves.

She grabbed the bottle of conditioner instead of the shampoo in the shower, and took ten minutes longer in the shower to fix that mistake.

At breakfast, she poured orange juice on her cereal instead of milk.

And as she walked out the door, she happened to look down at her feet and noticed she had on two different shoes.

She ran back inside, muttering at herself as she went.

"Caitlin?" her mom asked. "Is everything all right?"

She pointed to her feet. "Does this answer your question?"

Her mom put her hand to her mouth, trying not to laugh. "Oh, honey. I'm sorry. It's going to be okay. Whatever happens today, you know we're all proud of you."

Caitlin changed her shoes, then ran all the way to the bus stop, making it in the knick of time.

As she walked into school, she fiddled with the cute flower charm that now hung from the bracelet. Later, she would take it off and mail it to Mia. But she'd wanted to wear it just one more day. It had helped get her through her speech, and she knew it would help her get through a stressful day of announcements.

Esther was waiting for Caitlin at their locker. She moved aside so Caitlin could put her backpack and jacket inside.

"Hey," Esther said. "Cute clothes. Are they new?"

"Thanks. Yeah, we went to the mall on Saturday."

"Are you nervous?" she asked. "About the election?"

"I don't want to be," Caitlin said as she grabbed her notebook, a couple of books, and a pencil for homeroom. "But yeah, I am. I mean, it's fine if I don't win, you know? I just . . . I want to get it over with, I think."

"I understand," she said. "It's the way I feel about the

play. I might be a little disappointed if I don't get a part, but it's just the waiting and not knowing that's driving me crazy right now."

"That's exactly how I feel."

She shut the locker door and the two girls headed to class. As they walked, Caitlin spotted Tezra at her locker.

"Let's go say hi," Caitlin said.

They went over and Tezra gave each of them a hug. "I'm so glad to see you two. I wanted to tell you to come find me at lunch so we can sit together. I made cookies last night and brought some for all of us to share."

A warm, happy feeling washed over Caitlin. She'd brought cookies. To share!

"Ooh, what kind?" Esther asked. "I hope they don't have raisins. I hate raisins." Her hand flew to her mouth. "Oops, I probably shouldn't have said that. Now if they do have raisins, I'll feel really bad."

"Don't worry," Tezra said with a big smile. Caitlin noticed she had dimples in her cheeks when she smiled big and wide. "I made sugar cookies. You'll like them, I promise."

Caitlin rubbed her hands together. "I can't wait! Thank you for doing that. We'll see you at lunch, then."

"Yeah. And don't forget, after school the play assignments are going to be posted."

"Forget?" Esther said, laughing, "It's all I can think about."

Caitlin and Esther made their way to class. When they walked into homeroom, Mr. Hankins smiled and said, "Good morning, ladies. Caitlin, are you holding up all right?"

"I had kind of a rough morning," Caitlin replied. She looked over at Esther. "But everything's better now."

"Glad to hear it," he said. "The principal will be sharing all the election news during the morning announcements."

"Good," Caitlin whispered to Esther as they made their way to their seats. "Let's hurry up and get it over with."

Brie and her friends were whispering among themselves as Caitlin and Esther sat down. Maybe they were whispering about her and her silly speech, but Caitlin told herself she didn't care. No matter what happened, she'd found friends who liked her and accepted her. She was almost embarrassed now, thinking back to how badly she'd wanted to be a part of their little group, and why? What had they ever done to show Caitlin anything but how tight and exclusive their group was?

She looked over at Esther, who gave her an encouraging smile, just like always. Then she told Caitlin, "This is worse than going to bed with a tooth under my pillow, wondering how much money I'd get from the tooth fairy."

Caitlin grinned. "I know, right? Hey, did you ever wonder if you'd wake up and be surprised to find a ten-dollar bill?"

Esther nodded. "I even wrote the tooth fairy a note one time. It said, 'This tooth is very special to me. I'm really sad to be losing it. Can you please give me a lot of money so I won't be so sad?'"

"Did it work?" Caitlin asked.

"Are you kidding? I got a dollar bill, like I always did, with a note that said, 'Little girl, you should be glad you lost a tooth and not an ear.'"

The two girls laughed as the bell rang. A minute later, the principal came on over the loudspeaker. Caitlin squeezed the flower charm in her hand, her heart beating so hard, she wondered if Esther could hear it.

"I know you're all anxious to hear about our new student body officers, so I'll get right to it," Mr. Eckhart said. "I want you all to know I was very impressed with the speeches on Thursday. You're all winners in my book. All right, here we go. We'll start with the sixth grade. After tabulating the votes, we have D. J. Michaels for treasurer, Gina Tran for secretary, Kai Krokum for vice president, and . . ."

Caitlin held her breath.

"Our new sixth-grade president is Kristopher Barry."

A couple of kids in the classroom whooped and hollered, while others, including Brie and her friends, groaned.

"Congratulations one and all," Mr. Eckhart continued. "Now moving on to the seventh grade . . ."

"Sorry," Esther whispered, reaching over and giving Caitlin's arm a friendly squeeze.

"It's okay," Caitlin said, finally able to breathe.

Caitlin felt a tap on her shoulder. She turned to find Brie staring at her.

"I can't believe that," she told her. "You totally should have beat Kristopher. I mean, all that *Star Wars* talk? Come on, it's so last year."

"Oh. Well, thanks."

"I think you should run next year," Brie said. "I'd totally vote for you."

Caitlin shrugged. "I don't know. Maybe I will."

"Quiet, please," Mr. Hankins said.

They stopped talking and listened to the rest of the names. Esther passed Caitlin a note.

"It's way better you didn't win. Now you have a lot more time to read books. Our team is going to smoke all the other teams, just wait and see."

Caitlin really liked her new friend.

At lunch, they found Tezra. "I'm so sorry you didn't win," she said as the three girls sat down at a table together. "Are you doing okay? Is there anything we can do?"

"I'm fine," Caitlin said. "Really. My campaign wasn't that great. If I run next year, I'll do a much better job."

"We'll help you," Esther said. "We'll be your personal campaign team."

"That's right," Tezra said.

"Cool," Caitlin said, taking the sandwich out of her lunch bag.

"Here. Maybe this will make you feel better." Tezra passed Caitlin a big, round sugar cookie with the words *Proud to be your friend*. She passed one to Esther too.

"I figured whether you won or lost," Tezra explained, "it would be one hundred percent true."

"These are amazing," Caitlin said. "Thank you so much. Honestly, I'm just glad it's over."

"Now we wait for the last bell of the day to ring," Tezra said. "It's like they enjoy torturing us, you know?"

Caitlin gulped down a bite of her sandwich. She hadn't expected to win the election, and she wasn't that disappointed when she'd lost. But she suddenly realized if her two friends got a part in the musical and she didn't get anything, she was going to be upset.

Really upset.

Chapter 23

Crocus
Spring would be lonely without it

After school, the girls gathered outside the music room along with a bunch of other students. When Mrs. Sears stepped out, holding the cast list, the crowd buzzed with excitement.

"I'm so glad to see lots of enthusiasm for our musical," she told the students. "Tomorrow I'll hand out scripts to all of the students selected, and you'll want to start memorizing your lines right away. We'll begin rehearsals a week from today. Thanks to all of you who tried out, and please know, in some cases, it was a very difficult decision."

She taped the cast list to the wall and then turned and went back into the music room.

Caitlin hadn't cared that much about the election. After all, she'd gotten into it in the first place for basically all the wrong reasons. But the musical was different. She *really* wanted a part. As people pushed and shoved their way to the sheet, she found herself wishing really hard as she fiddled with the charm bracelet.

Please let me get a part.

Please let me get a part.

Please let me —

"Oh my gosh, I'm Fern!" Brie called out. "And Lavinia, you're . . ." Caitlin watched as she moved her finger across the cast list. "Templeton."

The four fun girls squealed, jumping up and down in celebration.

Caitlin looked at her friends.

"I wonder who got Wilbur," Caitlin said. "And Charlotte."

"Good for you," a kid said, "but can you move out of the way so we can see the rest of the cast?"

Caitlin felt sick. Lavinia had been really good. If she didn't get Charlotte, surely Caitlin didn't get it. There was no way Caitlin had sung better than Lavinia, especially with the silly snowman song. Was there?

The three girls inched closer and closer to the cast list, as kids read it and walked away, most with disappointment on their faces.

Finally, Caitlin had wiggled her way through the crowd so she was close enough to read the cast list. She looked back at her friends, who were looking at her with eager anticipation.

And in that moment, Caitlin realized it was time to do something for her friends for a change. Esther and Tezra had done so much for her during the campaign. It was time to give back a little bit.

So Caitlin scanned the sheet, from the bottom of the list going up, not looking for her own name, but the names of her friends.

"Tezra, you're the goose," Caitlin called out. "And Esther, you're the sheep!"

Caitlin watched as the two girls grabbed each other's arms and started jumping up and down. "We did it, we did it," they said as they jumped.

Caitlin was shaking as she turned around. This time, she went down the list from the top.

And there it was. Her name. After the kids who would play the various Zuckerman family members and Wilbur.

Caitlin's name was in the spot she had hoped and wished for.

"I'm Charlotte!" she squealed as she ran to her friends,

who had moved out of the crowd of people. "I can't believe it! My wish came true — I got the part I wanted."

As the three girls jumped around, hugging and laughing, Caitlin realized what a mistake it had been, worrying so much about the election, when it was the play she'd really wanted to be a part of all along. It was like the fun girls. She'd been so distracted, focusing on what she thought she wanted, she'd almost missed out on some great friends.

Thank goodness everything had worked out for the best, she thought. Just like her mom had said it would.

"We are going to have so much fun," Esther said.

"It's going to be awesome," Caitlin said.

"Wait until we tell Sonny," Tezra said. Her face drooped a little bit. "I just hope we can tell him soon."

"I hope so too," Caitlin said.

That night, another of Caitlin's wishes came true. Shortly after dinner, Caitlin received a phone call from Tezra.

"Hey," Tezra said. "I'm here at the soup kitchen. I'm using Mrs. Watson's phone. She had your home phone number saved. I couldn't wait until tomorrow to tell you. Guess who's back?"

"Sonny?"

"Yes!"

"Oh my gosh," Caitlin said. "Is he okay?"

"Yeah. He's a little weak. But he's doing fine. Mrs. Watson went and picked him up and brought him here for dinner. I told him about the two of us getting parts in the musical, and he's so happy for us. He said he'll definitely come and watch us."

"Please tell him I said hi. And that I'll see him on Wednesday, when we volunteer again. Thanks for calling and telling me, Tezra."

"You're welcome. See you tomorrow."

Caitlin spent the next hour making snickerdoodles. As they cooled, she went upstairs to her room. She took off the bracelet and wrapped it carefully in some tissue paper. Then she pulled out a piece of paper and started writing.

Dear Mia,

First of all, thank you SO much for sending that photo along. I ♥ it so much!

I'm really sorry about your foot. It sounds awful. I know it must be hard watching your friends play soccer while you have to sit on the sidelines. Maybe you can be the team's official photographer? At least you can take pictures, even if you can't do the other things you like to do, right?

As you'll see, I'm sending you some cookies I made tonight to hopefully cheer you up. I wanted to send you a fruit pizza, but it would have arrived a big mess that looked nothing like a pizza. I made one for my sister and her friends, and it turned out really good! They were so impressed, and they loved it as much as we did.

I'm also sending you the bracelet to wear next! I really hope you like the charm I picked out.

I was looking at my journal earlier today, thinking about how much has changed since I got home from camp.

The first week at school was so painful, because I was trying really hard to get in with one group of girls, even though I knew nothing about them. I just thought they looked cool and fun. Remember how my journal says, "BE UNIQUE, BE YOURSELF" on the front? It's like I'd forgotten everything I believed and was trying to be someone I wasn't just so I could try and fit in.

I've made two wonderful friends at school now. We're

in the school play together. And they cheered me up when I lost the class president election. (Don't worry, I'm not too upset about it.) And I am happy to say they like me for who I am.

The girl who is a miserable dancer.

The girl who enjoys poetry and likes to read.

And the girl who is crazy for flowers.

I hope you enjoy wearing the bracelet and the flower charm. Pretty flowers are like my Cabin 7 BFFs — they brighten up my life so much.

I know you're dying to know if the bracelet is lucky. I think you'll have to find out for yourself. I can say this: I feel super lucky to have so many great friends, and you are one of them.

Be happy! Sometimes awesome shows up when we least expect it. I know it's your favorite word, so I hope you get a whole bunch of awesome real soon!

Your Cabin 7 BFF,

Caitlin

Don't miss the next *Charmed Life*

Read on for a sneak peek!

Mia's hands shook with excitement as she opened the box. Inside she found a large baggie of homemade cookies, a letter, and something small wrapped in tissue paper. Her heartbeat quickened. She slowly peeled back the tissue, wondering if it might be the one thing she was really hoping for.

When she saw the charm bracelet, Mia let out a little squeal. Caitlin had chosen her to wear it next! She pulled the bracelet out of the paper completely and whispered, "Awesome," as she fingered the cute flower charm Caitlin had picked out. The bracelet no longer looked sad and lonely, the way it had the last time she saw it at camp. *Like a dog without a bone,* Hannah had said.

The thought made Mia smile.

She fastened it on her wrist and just like every other time one of the Cabin 7 girls had put on the bracelet, a camp memory came to mind.

In Mia's memory, the four girls, Mia, Caitlin, Libby and Hannah, had just gotten back from a trail ride. It was the first time Mia had ever been on a horse, and she'd enjoyed it up until the point where her horse, Jet, had stepped on a wasp's nest in the ground and gotten stung. All Mia had known at that point was that Jet flew off the trail and through the woods, giving his name new meaning. Mia had held on tightly, but when she had to duck to avoid a low branch, she lost her balance and fell to the ground with a loud *thud.*

She was okay, thankfully. But the barn wasn't exactly close by, so she'd had to get back on the horse and continue to ride the trail. Mia's three friends had been so kind and caring once they'd finally reached the end of the ride.

"Are you terribly sore?" Libby had asked her with her sweet British accent. "Shall we carry you to the cabin?"

Hannah, her southern friend, had given Libby a funny look. "Carry her? What is she, a sack of potatoes?"

Caitlin had stepped in and said, "Here, Mia. Put your arm around my shoulder and lean on me. Hannah, you're closest to Mia's size, get on the other side of her and do the same."

Mia had started to resist but changed her mind. They'd really wanted to help her, and so she had let them. Once they were back at the cabin, her friends had insisted she rest on her bunk until dinnertime. The next day, the soreness really hit. Fortunately, the camp nurse gave her ibuprofen, and it had helped with the pain over the next couple of days.

Now, Mia sighed. It was so nice to have a strong memory of camp, even if it wasn't her most favorite one because of the silly fall. She missed Camp Brookridge. More than anything, she missed her friends. Especially right now, when all of her friends at home were busy doing things Mia couldn't do. She looked down at the walking cast she wore and stuck her tongue out at the stupid thing. No soccer. No surfing. No nothing, it seemed like. How ridiculous that she'd fallen off a horse and managed to not break anything and yet, when she fell off a simple step stool at the café a couple of weeks ago, she'd landed funny and fractured a bone in her foot.

Confectionately Yours

Don't miss all the books in this delicious series!